OUT OF A CHRISTMAS SKY

OUT OF A CHRISTMAS SKY

A CARTERVILLE MYSTERY

ROBERT J. MCCARTER

LITTLE HUMMINGBIRD PUBLISHING

CARTERVILLE MYSTERIES

Each Carterville Mystery is stand-alone, but things do change in Carterville. The chronological order of the books are:

- **Out of a Christmas Sky**
- **Destroyer of Carterville**
- **The Blood of Carterville**
- **Faces of Carterville**
- **Return to Carterville**

Note: The events of this story take place seven months before *Destroyer of Carterville*.

PROLOGUE
6:52 AM CHRISTMAS MORNING. CARTER HILL.

I won't tell you that I hate Christmas, nor will I tell you that I love Christmas. My relationship with the holiday is much more complicated than that.

And getting more complicated all the time.

A dead body lying under a pine tree will do that. Especially when you're the chief of police and the victim is a friend of yours.

But we'll get to that. Let me set the scene first.

I can say that there is no better place to be than Carterville, Arizona for the holiday. Especially in the desert southwest. We are up between 6,400 and 7,100 feet in elevation with the 12,600-foot San Francisco Peaks towering behind us and covered in snow.

The little town with a population 293 is built on Carter Hill and is one of those historic western towns that started as a mining boomtown in the late 1800s and has a quaint feel with old red brick buildings lining the main street. Those buildings are now occupied by tourist-friendly shops.

And Christmastime in Carterville is Winterfest, the whole town decorated for the holiday with days of celebration, the population of Carterville briefly swelling from hundreds to thousands, the whole town taken over and transformed. All of it topped off by the Silver Ball, the big Christmas Eve bash.

The decorations go all the way to the top of Carter Hill, which sits at 7,100 feet in elevation and is crowned by ponderosa pine trees strung with green, red, and white Christmas lights that can be seen for miles.

The ponderosas turn to smaller piñon pines as you go down the hill with fir and maple trees over a hundred years old lining Main Street.

It's a steep climb up Carter Hill but worth the effort. Picture yourself there with every tree along the street strung with glittering Christmas lights, the old-fashioned streetlights wrapped in tinsel, the remnants of the last snowstorm still decorating the ground, and the towering peaks framed behind it.

It's like a perfect Christmas snow globe come to life and hard to imagine a better place to spend Christmas.

Except Carterville isn't just an old mining town turned quaint little tourist trap. Of the 293 permanent residents, 201 have some kind of power since the meteorite hit five years ago. But only while they are near Carterville. The zone of influence extends out about five miles and beyond that everyone is normal.

With all those powers, Carterville is a much better place for the strange and mysterious. And I should know. My name is Henry Carter. This town was named after my ancestor,

Samuel Carter, and I am the dutifully elected chief of police of this no longer quiet little town.

With the name and the badge, I feel kind of responsible for what goes on around here.

Christmas Day that year, the sky was clear and cold. The sun, being a lot luckier than I, wasn't up yet, but the fire on the horizon looked like a match being lit, yellow and orange and deep blue pushing the darkness back.

It was so beautiful it could bring a tear to your eye. Or that could be the cold, it was in the mid-twenties, my breath hanging in brief clouds of condensate with each exhale. Or maybe it was my hangover—the Silver Ball was last night and I had good reason to drink afterwards. Or the hour, it was early and I had no coffee in me. Or the fact that the victim had been alive and happy and flirting with me less than eight hours ago.

I took off my sunglasses, cheap aviators, so I could really see, and immediately regretted it. There was some snow on the ground, but not much. Just enough so the scarlet splatter of blood was shockingly stark. Lila Chang was lying there on the top of Carter Hill under a couple of ponderosa pines dressed like an elf with a dark green smock, red and white striped stockings, a long-sleeved red shirt, and those silly shoes and hat with their tiny bells. Her skin was pale, her limbs akimbo, her eyes open to that deep blue sky, but the lights clearly off.

Oh, and her throat had a puncture wound of some sort, thus all the blood.

I know red is one of the colors of Christmas, but when it's soaked into crusty old snow it doesn't seem that festive. And when the scent of blood, that sharp iron-tinged smell, is in the air, well, it's enough to make you want to never see red again.

"This ain't good, Chief," Officer Martin Lester said from behind me.

"No shit," I replied. There was no need to hide my annoyance from Lester, and no one else was here. The only building at the top of the hill is the old Carterville Church set just back from the lookout. Sitting in the parking lot that served the church and the overlook was the tent that was used for last night's Silver Ball. But it was early yet and no one else was here.

The view up here is spectacular, particularly in the winter with the inner basin of the San Francisco Peaks in one direction and the vast desert all the way to the Grand Canyon and beyond in the other. The snow disappearing as the desert took over from the mountains, the white melting into the tan, taupe, and salmon layers of the desert. The cut in the desert that marked the Grand Canyon clearly visible on a morning this cold and clear.

"Too late for Smitty to help," he said, stating the glaringly obvious, and with everything else it just made me grind my teeth.

A lot of the powers that residents of Carterville acquired the night the meteor hit are odd or small. But not Winston "Smitty" Smith, he had what could be called a real live superpower. He could heal people, although there was a price he had to pay which was why his blond hair was going grey in his early thirties.

But Smitty couldn't bring back the dead, thus Lester's statement of the stupidly obvious rubbed me the wrong way.

I inherited Lester from the old chief of police. He's been

on the job for twenty-five years and knows Carterville as well as anyone, but he never worked in a bigger city, and I think that the way things changed five years ago when the meteor hit and folks got powers made the job a little too much for him.

He was great when Carterville was kind of like Mayberry, but now that it was more like Stephen King's Castle Rock, he was out of his depth.

I glanced up at the older man. He was tall, and except for a slight bulging around the middle, still lean well into his fifties, his eyes sunk into his long face, a frown hanging below his prodigious steel grey mustache. That mustache, just like Lester, belonged to another era.

It was early and he had been on call and was woken up for this so he wasn't in uniform, dressed in jeans and a faded brown Carhartt jacket that was too big for him and kind of made him look like he was wearing a big paper bag. Wisps of his thick grey hair peaked out from underneath his black cowboy hat.

"Tell me again," I said, looking back to the dead elf in the snow, my stomach twisting, my teeth clenching more against my anger and guilt than against the cold.

"Dispatch in Flag woke me up," he said. "They got a 911, some woman sayin' there was a dead elf on top of Carter Hill. They traced the number, but it belonged to a burner phone. Walked up here and found her. Called you." He shrugged as if the gesture could somehow make up for the lack of detail and emotion in his report. But that was Lester, he was a man of few words. A quiet sort.

Lila's body—I'm not going to use the word "corpse" since this was someone I knew and cared about—was a few yards away under the trees. She was slumped against the dark brown bark, her head pointed towards us, her lifeless eyes accusing.

The Christmas lights were still on, a cheery green starting a few feet above her body, the cord snaking around the tree right behind her head. The incongruity was almost too much to bear.

Lester and I stood on the road and only one set of tracks led to Lila. The blood had dripped down over the green of her elf costume and onto the snow, but there were no drips of blood along the path she walked and no murder weapon visible.

"Powers," I said with a sigh.

"Yup, Chief," he said, his voice low like he was saying something profound. "It don't make much sense unless powers were involved."

I stood there staring, my hands shoved into the pockets of my jeans. I had left so quick I had forgotten gloves. I felt this rumble happening deep inside me. Part of it was the cold, my body wanting to shiver against it, but a lot of it was anger.

Lila was my friend and someone had killed her. This was my town and someone had been killed here.

And along with that quaking anger was a heavy load of guilt. Lila, while she was flirting with me last night, trying to pull me out of my funk, wasn't quite normal. She was fidgety and distracted.

I had missed something. I could have stopped this if I hadn't been caught up in the funk of yet another breakup with Annie Smith.

Lester stood there staring at the body like that was all

there was to do. And then I realized I was doing it too. The fire of my anger woke me up and I started barking orders.

"I'll stay with Lila. You go wake up Annabelle, tell her to load up the SUV and haul the CSI gear up here. Then go and get Doctor Lion, we'll need her to tell us what happened. And bring Mary Reilly too. The town is stuffed with tourists and word of this will spread and we'll need her help keeping the crowd away. I'll call the sheriff's office and let them know what we're dealing with. We might need extra bodies for this one."

After my little speech, a cloud of condensate hung in the air between the older man and me slowly dissipating while he just stood there, his dull blue eyes vacant, looking at Lila's body.

I was about to yell at him when the slight quiver of his chin stopped me. I had done my time in the Tucson Police Department. I had seen some things. But not Lester. And everyone loved Lila. With her bright smile, petite form, and happy disposition, she was the perfect person to play an elf.

"We'll get whoever did this," I said quietly. "I promise you that."

He nodded slowly, his haunted eyes fixed on Lila's body.

"Now go, Martin," I said. "I need you today. I need you to be at your best."

He bit his lower lip, sniffed, and nodded.

PART 1

BEFORE: CHRISTMAS EVE

ONE

TWENTY HOURS EARLIER, 8:13 AM
CHRISTMAS EVE. CARTERVILLE INN.

WHAT DO I HATE ABOUT CHRISTMAS? BESIDES FINDING A DEAD body under a tree on Christmas morning? Well, we could be here all day for that one, but let me say that I hate that it has become this gluttonous, consumeristic frenzy, this sinful celebration of the birth of a savior.

What do I love about Christmas? Mostly that my mother loved it and it was a time for the Carter family to gather and eat and drink and be merry. I also like the pagan roots of the holiday, a time to celebrate the days getting longer and the cold beauty of winter and the promise of spring to come.

I basically like the family and feasting part of it, and I hate the gift giving and the consumeristic part of it. I will admit that I'm just about the world's worst gift giver. It's just not in my DNA. There is all this pressure to do it, to find the perfect gift, and knowing that I'm going to fail just makes me grumpy.

That Christmas Eve, the morning before we found Lila's

body, I woke up from a deep sleep and stretched and groaned like some old cat, not remembering what day it was. I was in the Carterville Inn and Annie Smith, my on again, off again girlfriend, was not in bed with me.

Annie runs and lives in the Carterville Inn.

And here is where this gets strange for me as I write this. When I first write about someone, do I tell you their name, occupation, and power as if that is what matters the most? Do I sneak it into this memoir when their power becomes relevant—for the record, Annie's already has.

It feels strange. A person is not just their powers in the same way that they are not just their jobs. When I'm away from Carterville—rather rare—and introducing myself in a social setting, if I say, "I'm Henry Carter, the chief of police of Carterville, Arizona," I see the wheels turn in their heads.

First, that I live in that weird town they've heard all the strange stories about and probably don't believe.

Second, that I'm a cop so they better behave.

Third, they want to know what my power is and want me to do a trick for them like a trained dog. Everyone seems to have trouble understanding that the effect of our powers is in and around Carterville only. And they expect the powers to be big and flashy, not quiet and quirky like they usually are. I blame it on the never-ending supply of superhero movies and TV shows.

Okay, so this is my story to tell so I'm going to only talk about someone's power when it's relevant to what's going on. Just like I wouldn't mention that some could, say, juggle five balls at once, unless it was important to the story I was telling.

So I woke up in a hotel room in a historic building right on Main Street. I was on the third floor, the ceilings high and covered in the original stamped tin with an intricate pattern that reminded me of a Celtic knot.

I had slept the best sleep of my life. Because Winterfest just gives me a headache and I had asked for Annie's help. That's her power. People around her sleep well, but if she puts some effort into it, they have the best night's sleep of their lives. The kind where you wake up feeling awake and alive and ready to take on the world.

Annie and I had a brief thing in high school and she and I had gotten back together after my divorce some thirty-odd years later.

"Merry Christmas, baby," Annie said. She had a present in her hand, and I suppressed a groan and focused on how little she was wearing. Just a short black robe that was loosely tied and hung open almost to her navel.

Annie was a slim five-foot-four of fierce confidence. Piercing blue eyes, high cheekbones, and midnight black hair. Even at this time of year she had a pretty good tan going on.

She's also in the hospitality industry and is a world-class gift giver. The package she held was fairly large and perfectly wrapped in deep blue paper with gold and lighter blue Christmas trees. It was elegant and adult and all Annie.

I sat up, rubbing my eyes, the covers falling down. I yawned, mostly to buy time and pulled up the covers to hide my expanding waistline.

The decades hadn't changed Annie much physically, except for the crow's feet perched around her eyes and her deepening frown lines. Not so much for me. Where my mousey brown hair wasn't marching back from my forehead, the grey was getting a good foothold. And my middle was bulging out more the deeper I got into middle age.

I was just shy of fifty and it showed.

"You shouldn't have," I said, and I meant it.

She smiled, her eyes intense as she put the present on my lap and sat on the bed. I had the feeling like I was in the Olympics and I was about to be scored on my performance. I had felt this way with my ex-wife, so it wasn't just Annie.

"I know you hate the whole gift thing," she said with a smile. "I don't expect you to get me anything."

I didn't believe her, but I smiled back. While she knew a lot about what people wanted because of running this inn for so long, I knew a lot about when people were lying, having been a cop pretty much my entire adult life.

But relationships need their lies, right? Smooths over the potholes of being human.

"Thank you," I said, levering myself over and kissing her. I transitioned that into getting out of bed, sucking in my gut, of course.

"Aren't you going to open it?" Annie asked sweetly.

I was halfway to the bathroom, which was only a step from the bed. The rooms are small, with lovely antique furniture and photography of the area hanging on the walls.

"It's not Christmas," I said.

She shrugged, and the way the silk of her robe slid over her curves was quite distracting. "I know. Your family was traditional. No Christmas Eve presents. But there's a reason I want you to open this up today."

I stared at her and she looked away. Annie Smith is many things, but she is rarely shy. I sucked my gut in further and got back on the bed and hefted the gift. It was fairly light, something moving slightly inside.

"Thank you," I said, and I meant it. I slowly unwrapped the

paper knowing Annie would probably want to reuse it if she could. It was just a plain cardboard box, no clues there. Inside was a mass of tissue papers.

I paused, worried it was some kind of tchotchke that I'd hate and need to hang on the wall or have displayed for her to see when she comes over to my house.

Reaching in, my hands touched the softness of high-quality felt and I realized that Annie was too good at gift giving to saddle me with something I would hate. I smiled like a kid on Christmas Morning—which it almost was—and pulled out a brand-new cowboy hat.

It was a Stetson, cattleman style with a five-inch crown and a four-inch brim, made out of a high-quality silvery white felt.

Now let me tell you, buying a cowboy hat for someone who is serious about them is not a small thing. I'm not brand loyal, but not all cowboy hats are the same and the style is important. This one had a center trough and two indents on the side at the top. Perfectly symmetrical with a silver bead joining the hat band.

"I… It's…" I stammered.

While I wear a uniform, police blues, I also wear a cowboy hat. All the time. It's what Carter men do and have done since they came here over 130 years ago. It was a key part of my identity, and not only did Annie do good, she nailed it. The only surprise was the color.

"It's for the ball tonight," she said. She must have noticed my confusion.

And then it all made sense. Samuel Carter found silver under this hill… and some gold and titanium too. But mostly silver. The theme of our Christmas Eve celebration, the Silver Ball, was silver, and this hat was just perfect.

"I love it," I said, and most definitely meant it. "Thank you." I carefully moved the hat to the antique dresser and came back and kissed Annie soundly. She responded enthusiastically and one thing led to another—after a trip to the bathroom, I am a middle-aged man after all—and that's why I was late for work. And that's what set all of this madness in motion.

TWO

9:06 AM CHRISTMAS EVE. PEAKS GIFTS AND COFFEE.

CARTERVILLE IS A SMALL TOWN. WITH ALL THE GOOD, THE BAD, and the ugly that comes along with it. On the good side, I know everybody in town, every store, every street, every last pothole.

That's also on the bad side. This is the kind of town where we tend to form our own personal ruts and have a hell of a time getting out of them.

Annie and I, for instance. While our good times were excellent, our bad times were terrible. We got together about a year after my divorce, not long before the meteor hit, and had been doing our on again, off again thing since then.

The gift was fabulous, but it worried me. Our rut was when things got really good, when we were really on again, one of us would do something stupid and mess it up so we were really off again.

And the dummy that messed it up was usually me.

The hat was a world-class gift and I had nothing to give

her. Even though I was late for work, even though this was a day with too much to do, when I exited the Carterville Inn, I ignored the crystal clear blue sky, the spectacular view, and sucked in a cold breath of air and headed towards Peak Gifts and Coffee (we all call it PGC).

Main Street is a bit of a hodgepodge. Plenty of historic red brick buildings rising two or three stories intermixed with a few cinder block buildings and a few stick-built buildings built after the boomtown era or replaced after the fire of 1934.

PGC was one of my favorite places. Because it always smelled of coffee and because of the owner, Lila Chang.

Lila was all of five-foot-zero with bright brown eyes and an always bright smile. Since I just used the word "bright" there twice to describe her, I think that sums her up.

The old-fashioned bell rigged above the door rang when I entered, and I was greeted with a rush of heavenly smells and a thousand-watt smile from Lila.

"Coffee coming right up, Chief," she said.

She was behind the counter, somewhat hidden by the big stainless-steel cappuccino machine, but she had on her elf costume which was to be expected this time of year.

It wasn't some cheap costume, but handmade with a thick green smock, candy cane striped stockings, and hat and shoes tipped in tiny bells so she sounded like a fairy when she moved about.

If you wanted fancy coffee, PGC was the place. Not that I ever wanted fancy coffee. Or even cream and sugar. I wanted coffee strong and bitter the way God intended. It was a testament to the charming atmosphere and Lila's charisma that I got coffee here at all. Because it was that Americano stuff. Lila didn't have a drip coffee maker.

The shop was housed in a long, narrow space right in the center of town on Carterville Circle, the outer wall exposed red brick over a hundred years old and the inner one that separated her shop from the antique store next door was plain old sheet rock. There were three small tables up front by the big windows and Lila and her hissing, slurping machine was in the back.

The walls were hung with local art, mostly paintings, and the shelves were full of a shockingly wide variety of gifts (plenty of tchotchkes here). Things as simple as postcards, to genuine silver ore from what is left of the mine, to high-end jewelry, much of it fine silver made by the Hopi.

I loved the smell and I adored Lila, but the density of stuff just overwhelmed me. Especially today. When I felt the pressure of matching Annie's exquisite gift.

There were a couple of people I didn't recognize at the tables, so tourists, and a few more milling about the store. Arnold Hughes, the local insurance guy, was back at the counter getting coffee to go, something fancy that required a lot of slurping and hissing from Lila's gleaming contraption.

Hughes was tall and athletic, just over forty with a baby face and dark black hair just long enough to show off the bit of wave he had. His bangs were cut to a length that had him often brushing them back showing off his intense green eyes.

He was a confirmed bachelor, never married, and always seemed to be dating someone new. Usually from out of town.

I just stood there with my hands in my pockets feeling the newness of the beautiful cowboy hat perched on my head.

Worried about brushing something off the shelf with my equipment belt or my expanding belly.

And, yes, I should have gone shopping a lot sooner for Annie. And, yes, a man my age should have figured this kind of thing out long before. What can I say? I am a work in progress like every other human on the planet.

"Henry," Arnold Hughes said with a nod as he walked by me, his to-go coffee in his hand.

"Arnold," I replied in kind. He went by Arnie, but I'm not calling him Arnie until he calls me Chief.

I watched him go and dreaded this evening where he and his power would be on center stage at the Silver Ball. The guy liked the spotlight and he could probably sell life insurance to a dead guy. Not the kind of person I was wired to trust.

Someone cleared her throat behind me and I turned to see a real-live elf, or just Lila in her holiday getup. She was one of my favorite parts of the season.

"You're not just here for coffee," Lila said as she handed me a to-go cup of coffee, the smell even better close up. She was smiling, but this close I could tell it wasn't quite her normal smile. Her eyes kept darting away, looking at her customers.

She actually looked worried. The signs registered in my brain, but I was caffeine free this late in the morning and my mind was too filled up with my own problems.

"You a mind reader now?" I asked, shaking it off and doing my best to summon a smile.

She stepped back, her bells tinkling, and looked me up and down. Her shoulder-length black hair swished across her shoulders as she cocked her head to one side.

"That's it," she said with a smile. "You finally guessed my

power, Chief." She pressed two fingers to her right temple and squeezed her face into a comical mask of concentration.

I didn't know what Lila's power was, but I was pretty sure there was one. There were a few of us that claimed to not have powers, and Lila was one. And that was my fault. Mine wasn't the kind of power you made public. And since it's not relevant to this story, I won't be discussing it. Powers revealed can be used against you.

She blinked, her face resuming its normal configuration and looked me over again, her eyes landing on the new hat, which just made me uncomfortable.

Lila had a round face with a narrow nose and her eyebrows, when she was relaxed, were nearly a straight horizontal line. Her bangs rested at the line of her eyebrows, emphasizing them. There were some fine wrinkles around her eyes and mouth that told me she wasn't a kid, but I didn't know how old she was. She had one of those faces and was in the right span of years where it was honestly hard to tell. She wasn't young and she wasn't old, either. I would guess somewhere between thirty and forty.

She wasn't a Carterville native and got here about four years ago, a little before the meteor hit.

*Okay, okay, for you sticklers in the audience, I know that a hunk of rock from outer space that hits the ground is a meteorite not a meteor. But that sounds stupid, so I'm sticking with meteor.

Besides her age, Lila was a bit of a mystery. She never had family come visit and didn't talk about her life BC (Before Carterville). I could have pulled some background information on her and found out, but that would have just been rude. People get to have their secrets in my town as long as those secrets don't intersect with a crime or hurt somebody else.

"Annie gave you that hat," she said with a nod. "And now you are scrambling for a gift so you came to see your good friend Lila." She ended with her thousand-watt smile and an arched eyebrow.

"That settles it, Lila," I said with a laugh. "You are a mind reader."

She rolled her eyes like some teenager. "As if. I am just an astute observer of humans. My real secret is I'm an alien sent here to study your primitive species and send reports back to my galactic overlords."

I just blinked. Anywhere else on this planet you would be sure that she was kidding. But not in Carterville. Not since the meteor and the powers.

I'm not sure what configuration my face was in, but I don't think you had to be an astute observer of humans to see what was going on in my head.

Lila touched my arm. "I'm kidding, Chief. Come this way, I know just the thing for your Annie."

THREE

9:58 AM CHRISTMAS EVE. CARTERVILLE POLICE DEPARTMENT

My phone had been on mute and the battery on my radio had died. This meant all hell broke out when I walked into the Carterville Police Station, washing away the faint happiness that always lingers after an encounter with Lila. Or maybe it was the coffee. I was late getting my infusion of caffeine today and it felt good to be awake.

I had muted my phone because I needed to sleep last night and I wasn't on call. I know, a bad move, but sometimes you just have to unplug. Especially around Winterfest and the Silver Ball in Carterville. And then Annie had swooped in with the present as soon as I woke up and I hadn't thought of my phone.

"The mayor is in your office, Chief," Annabelle Unger said as soon as I walked in, the charm of her lovely southern drawl being swallowed by the urgency of her tone. "You're almost half an hour late and she's pissed."

Annabelle is a few years older than me and slim with

bright red hair streaked with purple. She was at the filing cabinets shoving paper in and wearing what I can only describe as an ugly Christmas sweater (and we best leave it at that) and her usual tight jeans and heels. She has been my dispatcher and office manager for years, but I have yet to get her to wear a uniform.

My adrenaline spiked. I had forgotten about my meeting with the mayor. This wasn't going to be a good day. I could just feel it.

I nodded and Annabelle's forehead furrowed quizzically and then her eyes went to my new hat and then a smile played across her bright red lips. "Y'all started Christmas early."

Our station isn't very big. It's basically one big room in the back of what was the original Carterville post office, a two-story brick building over a hundred years old. The front of the building was a bakery, so we were assaulted with the smells of baking bread and other sweets all day long, especially in the morning.

The main area has three desks, two littered with paperwork, whiteboards on the wall where recent calls are noted, and a bunch of filing cabinets. There are two holding cells in the back—Clint Ryan was in one still sleeping it off from last night. And finally there was the converted closet that was my office and the armory.

I'm not kidding about the closet thing. It's just wide enough to hold my craptastic metal desk and the locking cabinets for the deadly gear.

When I walked in and saw Carterville's mayor, Karen Winslow, I was sure this day was just going to keep getting worse. Her back was turned to me, but I could see that her thin shoulders were high behind her long, plaited braid of blond going grey hair.

My desk was at the back of the office facing out. Behind it was a tintype photo of Samuel Carter standing in front of the hulking Carter mine building, whose remnants are still on the other side of Carter Hill, made of big ponderosa pine trees.

The picture was there for many reasons. One of them was to piss off Karen Winslow, and if she had been in here staring at it for half an hour, this was going to be worse than I thought.

"I'm sorry, Karen," I said as I brushed past her, got to the other side of my desk, and hung my new hat on a hook on the wall next to the picture. "Busy morning. The battery on my walkie talkie died."

To emphasize, I pulled the walkie talkie out of my belt and shoved it in the charger on my desk.

"Not a problem, Henry," she said, but her pursed-lipped look said something else. She had the kind of face that seemed to naturally convey disappointment. At least when she looked at me.

I don't call her Mayor and she doesn't call me Chief. That right there kind of sums up our relationship and rivalry.

I've been chief a long time, a bit longer than she's been mayor, but the animosity between our families goes back over a century.

Karen's ancestor is Edward Winslow, the prospector that founded Winslow, Arizona. Back around 1900 there was some family drama and part of the Winslow family came to Carterville and tried to make it their own.

And to a large degree they succeeded.

The Winslows own most of the buildings along Main

Street and on Carterville Circle, and my sister and I, all that remains of the Carters here, only own a single house up on the hill.

Unlike most towns, the position of Chief of Police is an elected position and not one appointed by the mayor. This changed during Prohibition when a Winslow put a crony in the position and things got pretty Wild West around here with the speakeasies and a still around every corner.

Now it's a balance of power thing.

I got a whiff of her expensive and overly strong perfume as I sat down. It wasn't quite strong enough to erase the smell of horses, which I vastly preferred. She had a ranch not far out of town and it seemed that she liked horses a lot more than people, especially this time of year.

I leaned back and my old office chair creaked. "How many items on your list this morning, Karen?" I asked, giving her a smile with the leftover pleasantness of my visit with Lila.

"Thirty-six," she said, looking down at the clipboard in her hand.

She was a thin woman but tall. She wore what I would call a dress cowboy shirt in silver with pale blue embroidery and bits of metal at the tips of the collar. The collar was buttoned tight with a bolo tie that was a big hunk of turquoise surrounded by elegant silver.

She was this odd dichotomy of rough and ready western and monied elegance.

She didn't used to be this thin. A bout with breast cancer a couple of years ago had left her face looking a little hollow. They caught it late and it was bad. It took Smitty and his healing superpower to keep her alive.

And she wasn't kidding about the thirty-six items. Karen Winslow never kidded.

"Okay, then," I said suppressing a groan. "We're going to need Annabelle. I'll never keep it all straight."

Karen gave me a thin-lipped smile that spoke volumes. That she knew I would never keep it straight and that I was definitely the wrong man for the job in her eyes. Oh, and that I was about to pay dearly for making her wait thirty minutes.

This day was quickly getting out of control.

FOUR

7:18 PM CHRISTMAS EVE. THE CARTERVILLE INN.

What Karen Winslow needed me for was all security based. Our little town of less than three hundred was now in the thousands. The Silver Ball was when the rich and the famous came to visit Carterville.

The Carterville Police Department consisted of me, Officer Martin Lester, and Annabelle Unger. We used to have another officer, but that position had to be cut when the town council slashed my budget a few years before the meteor hit.

You'd think we'd really need that third officer. You'd think that the increased tourist traffic and bed board and booze tax could fund it, but then you'd be forgetting the Carter/Winslow rivalry. I suspect that Karen would happily cut Lester's position if she could, leaving me a chief of police without any police officers to supervise.

So during an event like this, the Coconino County Sheriff's Office loaned us a couple of deputies and we brought in private security.

Sure, Carterville looks just like some idyllic Christmas snow globe this time of year, but people are people and someone always makes trouble.

So I should explain Winterfest and the Silver Ball so this all makes some kind of sense.

At the bottom of Main Street, on the base of Carter Hill where things are relatively flat and the junipers dominate, we have a big parking lot for the tourists. There's parking along Main and on the side streets, but not enough. This time of year we have a couple security guards checking with vehicles before they are allowed up the hill.

From there it's shuttle busses and a lot of foot traffic up Main Street. All the shops are decked out with cheerful Christmas window paintings and carols play from outdoor speakers mounted to the decked out streetlamps.

Main climbs steadily about halfway up the hill to a point where the hill briefly flattens creating a wide terrace. The road briefly splits there into two one-way, one-lane streets that make up Carterville Circle. It's a roundabout that connects Main Street to Cedar Street, a really old one for Arizona, but we're not about to call it that.

The flat section is the center of town. Carterville Inn is here. PGC is here. The biggest tourist traps are here.

In the middle of the Circle is a sixty-foot-tall fir tree decked out in white lights and big silver ornaments. The street here is made out of pavers and this is where Carterville is at its most idyllic. When you walk the Circle, look into the shops, get glimpses of the peaks towering above and the desert below, you might think that it's some kind of perfect little small town somehow protected from the never-ending march of time and progress.

You'd be wrong, of course, but this is the illusion that the mayor and the town council and the merchants work so hard to create.

It's what Winterfest and the Silver Ball are all about.

After the brief interruption of the Circle, Main Street climbs the rest of the way up the hill, making one switchback on the steepest section of the hill and ending at Carterville Overlook, where the view cannot be beat. A big tent is set up in the parking lot and this is where the Silver Ball is held.

Yup, it's December, and at the top of the hill we are over seven thousand feet in elevation so the junipers are gone and it's big ponderosa pine trees and it's cold.

So there are those tall propane heaters inside and it's the kind of function where you just might wear your coat most of the time. Being a "ball" there is a sit-down dinner, dancing to a live band, and a very busy cash bar that specializes in hot libations.

So my day was rushing around from the top of the hill, to the Circle, to the bottom of the hill checking on security and traffic flow and interfacing with Officer Lester, the sheriff's deputies, and private security.

And my day got a late start, and Karen saddled me with extra tasks, and before I knew it, I was at the Carterville Inn picking Annie up for the ball. Ten minutes late, I might add.

My feet hurt. My head hurt. I was starving. But at least I had a beautifully wrapped present in my pocket.

I forgot all of that when I saw Annie. She was in a form-fitting, long-sleeved black dress, the bottom of it silver that twisted and blended with the black in a beautiful way. The waist was tight with a broad silver belt. Her long black hair was up in an elegant bun and diamonds glinted at her earlobes. She was just beautiful.

My jaw hung open and one of her eyebrows arched and she laughed. "You like?" she asked, a playful glint in her piercing blue eyes.

We were in the lobby of the Carterville Inn. It used to be a saloon (and brothel, of course), the reception counter being the original long wooden bar.

I nodded, still unable to speak. I wanted nothing more than to skip the ball, drag her back upstairs like some stupid caveman, and see what was under that dress. Like I didn't already know. Hey, don't blame me. Blame God, or evolution, or whatever floats your boat in that department. I didn't actually choose to be this way.

But I did have free will and a functioning cerebral cortex so I shoved those caveman thoughts down and pulled out the present and handed it to Annie.

It was perfectly wrapped in silky green paper with curled red ribbons. Cleary not wrapped by me. If I wrapped something, it still looked like a ten-year-old had done it with bad edges and way too much tape.

Her face lit up and that moment there, I never wanted to end. Annie's face is much more configured to frowning than smiling. The moments I've talked about here are the sweet, tender moments. But Annie can be a hellion, as I was about to be reminded.

"For me?" she asked.

I nodded again.

Her brow furrowed and the smile disappeared for just a moment as she tentatively took the gift. That was a warning sign, one that I missed. I blame it on the caveman thoughts and the aching feet and the low blood sugar.

Which is a convenient excuse. Much better than admitting that my emotional intelligence wasn't the best when it came to intimate relationships. I mean, I'm pretty good at my job so I know how people tick, but when it comes to the opposite gender, I am often still dumb as a thumbtack… or a caveman.

She leaned and sniffed the package delicately.

"PGC," she said quietly. Warning number two. I'm guessing she could smell the coffee.

"Yup," I said happily. "You're going to love it."

Her blue eyes narrowed briefly and met mine before she carefully put the package on the old wooden bar and unwrapped it, her movements careful and delicate. She moved tentatively, like she expected the package might be alive and might sting or something.

Still not in sync with what was going on, I just thought she liked the gift wrap and wanted to maybe reuse it.

When she pulled out the bracelet, she smiled big and then her face darkened, her mouth pulling down into a frown, making it clear that she had earned those frown lines.

It was a Hopi bracelet made of silver with a teardrop-shaped piece of polished turquoise in the middle. The stone had some streaks of blue that caught Annie's eyes nicely.

This wasn't the kind of jewelry Annie usually wore, but Lila had seen her admiring it and I trusted Lila.

"You were a busy boy this morning," she said, her tone light.

"Well…" I began with a shrug, quite aware of the beautiful new hat still perched on my head. "I'm not very good with the presents. Is it all right?"

"Lila picked it out, right?" she asked, her voice still soft.

I nodded. There was no use denying it.

"So, right after I got you that hat, you ran down to PGC and had Lila tell you what to get me?" Her tone was not so light anymore.

This was like the fifth sign and it finally got through my tired brain that this wasn't going to go well.

"You don't like it?" I asked, my brain still not quite engaged and my emotional IQ sadly lacking.

"That's not the point, Henry," she said, putting the bracelet back in the box and handing it to me.

"That I waited to the last minute?" I asked, trying to figure it out.

She sighed, shook her head, and rolled her eyes. Now I get that I'm not perfect, that I have flaws, huge ones, but that gesture of hers just set me off.

"Pretend I'm as stupid as you think I am, Annie," I said, folding my arms. "And explain it to me. In short sentences."

"How is this for a short sentence," she began, and I was really regretting saying that. "Lila Chang has a thing for you. And that's the woman you run to right after I gave you that hat. Right after we made love."

I just stood there blinking.

"Don't pretend you two don't flirt," she said, her cheeks reddening. "All the time. Don't stand there and tell me you don't go in there more often than you need to."

I opened my mouth but didn't manage to get any words out. I was fond of Lila. I did go into PGC more than I needed to. But was I flirting?

"And Patty Walsh down at the dinner," Annie practically spat out. "Little miss knows your every desire."

Patty had a power. She knew what you wanted before you asked for it. She was a waitress at the Carterville Diner and Annie wasn't completely wrong about her. I could see how the word flirt applied there.

"Lila has a thing for me?" I finally asked.

"Wake up, Henry," she said. "You're Henry Carter. You're the chief of police of *Carter*ville. And you're the heart and goddamn soul of this little town. Of course she has a crush on you. As well as Patty and at least three other women and one other man I can think of."

It was suddenly hot in here, my eyes roaming around the room as I took a step back. High ceilings with the same stamped tin as the room I woke up in. Old historic pictures of Carterville starting back in the late 1800s when it was a booming mining town. One of Annie's employees was behind the counter, a girl named Kennedy, her brown eyes wide as she watched us fight.

And yes, it's not lost on me that I stumbled back like a fighter who had just taken a teeth-rattling uppercut to the chin. It's kind of how I felt.

Patty has a crush on me? That's what was really messing with me. Patty with her long, curly red hair and distracting curves. Patty who knows what everyone wants before they ask for it. I had been the first person Patty had met when she moved here, not too long before the meteor hit.

"So," she continued, "when my man goes running to one of the women in town that fawns all over him the moment he leaves my embrace, and it's about me, it's kind of a problem, don't you think?" She stood staring at me, her hands on her hips.

"What?" I asked.

I bumped into an antique armchair and found that I was on the other side of the narrow lobby.

"You know what," she said, "something's come up. Kennedy has a family emergency and I have to stay here tonight. Enjoy the ball, Henry."

She turned and walked away from me, her steps fast, and I just stood there dazed while Kennedy stared at me.

Patty had a crush on me?

FIVE

8:23 PM CHRISTMAS EVE. THE SILVER BALL.

ALL MEN STILL HAVE THAT PROCREATION-OBSESSED CAVEMAN IN them, that primitive man whose actions are still largely guided by the more base parts of the brain. Or rather not so much the brain but the biological imperative to procreate and ensure the survival of the species.

I had done my part there. My son was down in Phoenix. He decided to stay down there even though college is out of session. He's in his "I hate the small town I was born in" phase. I was planning to drive down there on Christmas Day after all this madness was over and see him.

But just because I had done my part doesn't mean that the caveman in me, that my "lizard brain," wasn't still full of all those primitive, procreation-obsessed thoughts.

The next hour was a blur. Without Annie, I drove my old Toyota pickup to the overlook and checked in with Martin Lester, who was running things up there.

After seeing that everything was running smoothly, we

walked to the overlook and just stood there in the dark, the cold of the night reaching out its fingers and grabbing me. I stared out into the dark at the starry sky and just breathed. Trying to let go of the fight and all those silly caveman thoughts about Annie and how she was "mine."

Carterville is on the north side of the San Francisco Peaks. The light of Flagstaff is behind us and there are no major population centers to the north, at least not within a hundred miles. The moon hadn't risen, so it was about as dark as you can get.

The overlook is edged with a low wall made of local volcanic rock. There's a few of those hulking old-fashioned metal binoculars you feed quarters in. They're called tower viewers, I think. There were also a couple of picnic tables, all of it shadows in the darkness.

"Somethin' bothering you, Chief?" Lester asked.

I sighed. "I like the dark," I said, not answering his question. "It may not be calm, but it feels calm. You know?"

Behind us in the tent, music was playing and we could hear the mixed cacophony of voices and laughter underneath it. The smell of grilled meat wafted out, reminding me just how hungry I was.

"No, sir. I do not," he said.

I nodded to the north. "There's not much out there. Just the desert and the Grand Canyon and beyond that, the quiet of southern Utah. All bathed in darkness. Not many people out there, and most of the animals are settled in for the night. It feels calm out there. But it can hide all manner of chaos. Owls out hunting rats. Skunks foraging. Coyote hunting those skunks."

I looked at the tall man in the darkness, his long face

outlined in the temporary lighting we had set up in the parking lot and leaking from the tent.

"But you like it?" he asked, still looking out at the desert.

"Yeah," I said with a nod. "I need some calm now and then, even if it's only an illusion."

He turned, and while I couldn't see his eyes clearly, I could feel his gaze. "You and Annie fighting again?"

I chuckled, but it wasn't a happy sound. "That obvious?" I asked.

"When you didn't show up with her, yeah. And—" He turned away and stared back out into the darkness.

"And what?" I asked.

"It ain't my place," he said.

"What isn't your place, Martin?"

He shrugged and stared down at his feet as he kicked at the hard-packed dirt. "It ain't just the dark that hides things."

"Spit it out," I said, no longer enjoying the moment.

"Well… Ms. Smith got here while you were checking in with some of the security guys," he said slowly.

I felt a brief moment of lightness. Maybe Annie had come to her senses. Maybe she realized that Lila was just my friend and this was just a tiny bump in our long relationship. Annie and I had grown up together, we had known each other our entire lives. Maybe this would actually help us become closer if—

"And she wasn't alone," Martin added.

I sucked in a breath and stared out at the dark again, the lightness of hope twisting into the density of despair.

———

I DON'T UNDERSTAND WOMEN.

I don't.

Not at all.

Well, that is clearly an exaggeration. I understand certain things about them, about specific women, but in general I am clueless. Clearly, I am.

After the cold of the night, the modest heat of the tent hit me along with the noise of the crowd, the clinking of silverware on china, and the smells of grilled meat and vegetables.

The band was done with their first set and dinner was mostly over.

It didn't take long to spot Annie. She was hanging on the arm of the tall and athletic Arnold Hughes and laughing in an over-the-top kind of way on the other side of the tent. The two of them were in a group with Karen Winslow and her husband Ken Fischer, Winston "Smitty" Smith, and a few town council members.

Arnold Hughes was younger, fitter, handsomer, and a lot better off than me. Full head of hair to boot, still a sleek, dark black. He was on the town council and a reliable ally of Karen Winslow. Yeah, not much love lost between the two of us. Seeing him with Annie hanging off of him highlighted his physical advantages over me in a way that just made me feel hollow.

I will say that if I was being completely logical about this, he was a much better match for Annie than I am. Boring as hell, I am sure, but a better match.

Smitty's presence made it an even less desirable location for me. The town healer was dressed in his flowing, new age clothing. Not silver, but bright white like he was trying to portray a level of purity that I knew he didn't have. I had arrested him multiple times. His sharp features and the grey invading his scraggly blond hair made him look a lot older than he was. The bigger the power the bigger the price, it seemed. Not much love lost there either.

As an elected chief of police, I am in part a politician. Not willingly, I might add. That group of city leaders was where I should be going. They controlled much of my budget which there was never enough of since the meteor hit.

But I didn't do that. There was just no way. I caught Annie's eye, tipped my beautiful new hat to her, and I went to the bar.

Lila Chang was there serving up drinks in her adorable elf costume. So much the better.

Yup. I don't always make things easy on myself.

"Hey, Chief," she said as I leaned against the tinsel and Christmas light bedecked bar. One of those portable units on wheels. "You okay?" Her thin chin nodded towards Annie and Arnie, her face pulled down into an unusual frown.

Oh, lord. Annie and Arnie. Their names are cutely alliterative. Perhaps they are destined to be together.

"Nothing a little gin and soda won't cure," I said. I shrugged and added, "Or a lot of gin and soda."

Annie choosing to do this so publicly would set tongues wagging all around town and made any future reconciliation that much harder.

I watched as Lila deftly poured the drink, remembering the lime and the dash of bitters that I prefer.

The frown stayed on her face and her eyes kept roaming to the group of revelers that included Annie and Arnie.

God. I can't stand it. "Annie and Arnie." They probably deserve each other.

"You need a drink too?" I asked. The bar was unusually quiet, a brief lull in traffic, and Lila seemed upset. I took a sip of my drink, letting the alcohol start to unwind the knots in my shoulders.

"Old money bags just raised my rent," she said, referring to Karen Winslow. "Again. Third time this year."

"Third time?" I asked.

Lila leaned against the bar with a sigh. "Yeah. Some shit went down earlier in the year so I negotiated a lower price on my lease, but the new contract came with some clauses I didn't quite understand. Like raising my rent by ten percent every quarter."

She looked around, making sure we were alone and lowered her voice and leaned closer. "Emily next door has a good lease, but old money bags has offered to let her out of it and is dragging her feet on repairs."

"What? Why?" I asked.

This is a small town. Everyone knows everyone's business. But Karen was clearly up to something that hadn't crossed my radar.

"The Carterville Brewery," Lila whispered, and then a couple of tourists came up to the bar.

Carterville, quite surprisingly, didn't have a brewery. Lila's and Emily's shops were in the right location, right on the Circle. Knock out the wall between them and the shop on the other side of Emily's and you'd have enough space.

Our conversation was interrupted by Karen Winslow stepping up onto the band's stage taking the mic.

"Thank you all for coming," she began, and I suppressed a groan. Time for the speech. Time for the Carterville freak show to begin.

The Silver Ball was not cheap. The attendees were a mixture of about half locals, mostly business owners with money, and about half tourists. And the tourists came knowing that they'd see something amazing.

I looked at Lila and she rolled her eyes and I laughed. The mayor rattled on about what a perfect and wonderful place Carterville was and how grateful we all were that all these wonderful people had come to spend Christmas here, and how delighted we were to share a taste of what made Carterville the most special.

The speech was so saccharine I practically got a cavity from it.

And then it was time for Arnold Hughes to be handsome and charming and to dance the way only he could. As the band started up again, he pulled Annie out onto the dance floor, twirled her around, pulled her close, and with a giggle, they rose six inches into the air.

There were gasps from the tourists and a lot of phones recording.

My jaw clenched for multiple reasons.

First, Annie looking gorgeous in her black and silver dress, a smile lighting up her face as she danced with the younger, handsomer, more athletic Arnold Hughes.

Second, this ill-advised demonstration that I had argued against. Carterville powers were known, there were lots of articles and rumors, but as a rule we didn't show off our powers. We didn't talk about our powers. And we certainly didn't perform like trained animals.

The murmur of voices competed with the band as the tourists gawked. I was happy to see I wasn't the only local with a scowl on their face.

Since Hughes's power is important, now is the time to talk about it. It's levitation, plain and simple. He can move himself up and down in the air, defying gravity. And unlike Annabelle Unger, who had a similar but weaker power, his was pretty major.

He and Annie rose about eight inches into the air and continued to dance, but in an unusual way. He was stationary with their hands joined as he twirled her around him, her movements tugging him slightly this way and that. Their hair didn't float away like they were weightless or anything, it was just like he stood on an invisible floor, or really, a narrow pedestal while Annie giggled and swirled around him.

And how the hell was I going to compete with that?

I finished my drink and turned back to Lila who had an unusually sour look on her face as her dark eyes watched the two of them. "I think I need another," I said.

She blinked, as if she had been somewhere else, and nodded.

———

"Come on, Chief," Patty Walsh said, gently taking my arm.

I was two drinks down and Lila was making me a third, all on an empty stomach. And Lila hadn't been stingy with the gin, so I was starting to feel it.

The band was playing and people were dancing. A lot of ladies, and a few men, had taken their time floating in the air with Arnold Hughes, and now the dreaded Annie and Arnie were at it again, this time floating higher, a good three feet in the air so no one could miss them. The man didn't even appear to be self-conscious about the spectacle which made me just want to go hit him. Well… and that he had Annie in his arms and giggling again.

Patty's interruption was well timed and welcomed. I smiled at her, my eyes widening a bit. She was wearing a glittering silver dress, her wavy red hair cascading over her shoulders. No dye there with just a few random strands of grey taking hold.

She was beautiful. Not in the way of Hollywood, but in the real live girl next door kind of way. Freckles perched on her cheeks. Lovely green eyes. Generous feminine curves.

And she had a power. She knew what everyone wanted before they asked for it. Although, tonight, I doubted that she knew what I wanted, because I sure as hell didn't.

Except another drink, of course.

"You look beautiful," I said as I smiled at her.

"Thanks, Chief. Now come with me," she said.

"Sure, I just need my…"

Patty grabbed the drink from Lila and walked away. I had no choice but to follow her. And the view was pleasant, I must say. And since I was in the state I was in (and it wasn't just the alcohol), I said it. "God, you are really beautiful, Patty."

She didn't say anything, and I couldn't see her face, but I like to think that she was smiling.

She led me back behind the bar through a curtained area and into another tent that held all the catering supplies which at this point looked like a bomb went off with bins full of plates, warming trays without food on them, and a few waiters standing around.

I could smell the lingering scent of steak mingling with

something buttery and something sweet. My stomach grumbled but I was still more focused on the drink in Patty's hand.

At a long table, Big Frank Paulson was hunched over fussing over cheesecake, dusting silver sprinkles on top of the dollop of strawberry compote that rested on top.

Frank was a big man, at least 250 pounds, with a shaved head and the kindest blue eyes you've ever seen. He wore his ever-present white apron over jeans and a simple blue T-shirt. Frank was also my best friend. We went to high school together and the only thing that has ever come between us was Annie Smith. He dated her first when we were all teenagers.

I just watched as Frank worked, his concentration complete. He ran the Carterville Diner, and while he would never call himself a "chef," he was an amazing cook.

After the waiters began hauling the desserts off, Frank took one of them and brought it over to me. "Eat," he said, his round face pulled into a frown.

I suddenly remembered how hungry I was. Had I even eaten today? The morning with Annie just set the day off kilter.

I looked at Patty, her arms crossed and her eyes serious. "Eat," she echoed.

So I ate while the two of them silently watched. And then Patty came up with some bread and butter so I ate that. And then some cold mashed potatoes, so I shoveled those in. I honestly would have eaten just about anything at that point, the two of them just silently staring at me while the wait staff swept in and out taking the desserts out.

"Better?" Patty asked.

I nodded and then sighed. With food in my belly I was less

caveman and suddenly very sad. Annie and Arnie. Their two stupid names only one letter apart and utterly perfect for each other.

"What happened?" Frank asked.

I pointed at my hat. "My Christmas present from her." I shrugged. "I panicked and had Lila help me pick something out for her, and—"

"You're telling me Lila picked it out," Patty said, interrupting me.

I nodded.

"Shit, Henry," Frank said. "That was stupid. And you guys broke up?"

I shrugged again. "We had a fight. She said she didn't want to come tonight. It took her five seconds to find another date. I am not aware of an official breakup."

They both just stared at me. Patty had put my drink down on one of the tables and I so wanted it, but I had a rule against getting drunk in public. I don't find my own self-pity something I want to share. This disaster was far too public as it was. And I was on duty so I shouldn't have been drinking at all.

"What are you going to do?" Frank asked.

I shrugged yet again. "Get some coffee. Go do my job."

SIX

10:12 PM CHRISTMAS EVE. THE SILVER BALL.

I swear the tension between Annie and I was visible. Sparks erupting as our hands clasped, as I grabbed her waist and pulled her close.

Arnie hadn't wanted to let me cut in, but I am the guy wearing a gun and taser on my belt dressed in a blue uniform and that does engender some respect on occasion.

"Are you having a nice evening?" I asked, pulling her into a simple two step. The beat was too fast for it, some old Eagles song, but it's what I could do and not look like a fool.

I had done my schmoozing, talking to some council members, keeping it light, slipping in some of the challenges the department was facing. It was the end of the night and it was time for a bit of clarity from Ms. Annie Smith.

"Yes. Lovely," she said. "And it looks like you and Lila have had a nice evening too."

I clenched my jaw to trap in the words that wanted to leap out. I swallowed and said, "Lila is just a friend. And I will give you that she wasn't the best choice tonight for me just like your time with Arnie wasn't the best choice for you."

"Time will tell," she said with a smile so sharp it could draw blood.

We moved amongst the crowd, the two step and oddity amongst the more free-form moves of some of the other dancers. Karen Winslow was being twirled under the arm of her husband Ken and I saw her eyes following us. I'm sure many others were staring too. Small towns need something to talk about and I am sure we were the big story making tongues wag tonight.

"It will indeed," I said. "I am curious, though, since you seem to be dating someone else. Did we break up?"

"Why?" she asked. "You looking for a late night rendezvous with Lila? Or maybe Patty. Seems like she's what it took to get your attention away from Lila."

"Jesus Christ, Annie. Lila is a friend. Besides, I'm way too old for her."

"She just turned forty," Annie said with another one of those sharp smiles. "Seems like if you were her 'friend' you would know that."

I sighed. I had no idea she was that old. And then I was stricken with this strange guilt. I was a middle-aged white guy and I couldn't even guess the age of a woman of Asian descent. And wouldn't I have known she just had a big birthday if we were friends? Maybe we are just friendly and not friends. There is a difference, a big one.

"Annie, please," I said. "I'm begging you to believe me. There is nothing there. I am with you, at least I thought I was."

"And Patty?" she asked, that sharp smile plastered on her

face. I know it's only metaphorical, but I felt like I was bleeding. "Nothing there?"

How the hell was I supposed to answer that? Patty was an ideal, a dream. A woman that knows what you want before you even ask for it. Patty and I were really friends. I knew she was a high school art teacher before she came here. She loves jazz and is an amazing painter. She has a cousin in Phoenix and was headed there after a bad divorce and just stopped in Carterville for food and decided to stay.

"Patty and I are friends," I said.

"You seem to have a lot of *friends*, Henry," she said as we two-stepped across the floor. I kept us away from the band, I needed to be able to hear her, keeping us towards the edge of the dance floor close to the tall propane heaters, which were making me sweat.

The song was going to end soon and I was running out of time.

"I'm the goddamn chief of police. It's my job to know the people of this town," I said through gritted teeth. "What the hell do you want from me?"

"The truth," Annie said. "How many of your 'friends' do you have feelings for?"

The song ended and it was relatively quiet. Couples parted but Annie and I kept standing there, our two hands clasped, my other hand on her waist. Arnie was staring at us, looking like a lost puppy dog, and I could feel other eyes on us.

"How many?" Annie repeated, her voice loud in the relative silence. "It's a simple question."

"I have feelings for you, Annie," I hissed. "That is all that should count."

She smiled, the sharpest one yet, and said, "Thank you for

the dance, Henry." She swirled around and went back to Arnie.

I was left with a whiff of her perfume and a gnawing emptiness in my belly that had nothing to do with hunger.

———

I KNOW PEOPLE IN CARTERVILLE HAVE "POWERS." THE KIND YOU might capitalize. But everyone has powers. Abilities that seem extraordinary.

Lila seemed to have the natural power of contagious happiness. I always felt happier, or less sad at least, when I was around her, and I know it wasn't only me. Martin Lester was a freakishly good marksman for no reason that I could tell, it's not like he practiced much. If anyone should be taking care of horses, it was Karen Winslow. They just seemed to be calmer around her.

I sometimes think that the meteor that gave us the capital-P powers just enhanced what was already there. Made us more of what we already were.

Patty Walsh was already an empathetic person so she now knows what people really want.

Annie, despite her sharp edges, really likes to take care of people, and now she can help them sleep.

There are exceptions, of course. Winston "Smitty" Smith used to be a part-time mechanic and a full-time petty thief and now he can heal people, like he did Karen Winslow and so many others. But maybe that fits too. He uses his power to extract money and power from those around him. His thieving is no longer petty, but he's still a thief.

And now you are all wondering what my power is. What

would a life-long cop's power be? My power doesn't come into play in this story, but it does in others. I'll spill the beans eventually, but not yet.

And, no, I don't give a damn about storytelling conventions. These are my stories, the stories of Carterville, and I'll tell them any way I like.

I guess writing about this stuff has taken me back to the feelings I was having that night. Grumpy doesn't even begin to cover it.

You see, I loved Annie. With all the complexity that two humans who had known each other for forty-some-odd years bring to the table. Who had been together and been apart. First in the desperate longing and passion of youth and then in the wiser and cooler passions of middle age. But passions nonetheless.

I loved how sure of herself she was. Or seemed to be. I loved how deeply she felt and how unafraid of her emotions she was. Or seemed to be. I loved her petite physical form and how when she touched me, I felt like the teenager I was when we first found our passion. My protruding belly seemed to melt away and I was no longer worried about my retreating hairline or invading army of gray hairs.

This was Annie's natural power over me. Or maybe a natural power between us. If we were single, we seemed to find ourselves together, despite the challenges.

And I knew Annie. I accepted her for what she was. Isn't that what love is? What was this crazy jealousy of hers? Yes, I was very fond of Lila, but no longer knew if she was actually a friend. Thanks a lot for that doubt, Annie.

And I was deeply attracted to Patty, but let me refer you to previous musings about cavemen, and lizard brains, and biological imperatives. God and/or evolution made me this way.

Yes, I may sometimes think and feel like a caveman but I wasn't doing anything about it. And isn't that the whole point of civilization?

I was slumped on a chair in the mostly empty tent at the Carterville Overlook. The tables were a chaotic jumble of dirty dishes and glassware. On the other side of the tent, Frank's catering staff was clearing it, the black-uniformed people looking like fish nibbling away at something. The heaters were off and it was getting cold.

Martin Lester was slumped in a chair next to me. He had just updated me on a few security matters and we had lapsed into silence.

That'll happen with someone like Lester who's not all that talkative, and besides, we've known each other for my entire life. There's just not much small talk left.

I was exhausted, underfed, and regrettably sober. I wanted nothing more than to cover these thoughts and feelings with a good gin buzz, but I was still on duty.

Well… not really. The ball was over. I could go home, but after seeing Annie leave with Arnie, I just couldn't summon the energy.

"I'm gonna git," Lester said as he roused himself.

I nodded. "Have a good Christmas," I said. With all the tourists in town we both had to work tomorrow, so it's not like it's a relaxing holiday or anything, but it is what you say.

"You too, Chief." He was standing, his hands shoved into his pockets, his jaw hanging open making his face look longer than it was. "Sorry about… you know…"

I smiled and it wasn't completely fake. "Thanks. Much appreciated. Go get some sleep."

Lester stood there for a moment, restless, his eyes darting around the tent. But only for a moment, and not long enough to reach through my funk. He soon turned and was gone.

As I was slumped there, my eyes unfocused, I watched the school of people nibbling away at one table and then another, as they hauled empty tubs in and then swept out with them full. With the clanging of dishes and the murmur of voices it was almost relaxing.

The place had this strange mélange of scents. Food, spilled beer, sweat, all of it being suppressed a bit by the cold.

"You need this," Lila said as she plopped herself down next to me and put a drink in front of me. It was a short plastic cup with clear liquid, a lime slice, and a reddish substance mingling in with the ice and liquid. Gin and soda with lime and a dash of bitters.

Lila was still in her full elf regalia, so the tiny bells tinkled as she sat down.

She must have seen my eyebrow raise because she had an identical drink. She shrugged, "I really shouldn't be drinking —I've got to work in the morning—but I know you are obsessed with these and I'm curious."

She held her cup up and we touched the plastic together and we each took a sip.

Her face contorted a bit and I had to laugh.

"Yeah, I don't know about gin and lime together," she said.

I shrugged. "More for me then."

Her face relaxed and she nodded towards the empty dance floor. "Sorry about all of that."

I shrugged. "It's what Annie and I do."

Her forehead furrowed and her eyes darted around. It was a brief moment but was quickly replaced with her ever-present smile. She reached over and gently touched my arm, her smile turning tender. "You deserve better."

I should have asked her what was going on. I knew she was stressed about Karen Winslow raising her rent, but there seemed to be something else. But I was too tired and too focused on my own drama. And I was too shocked by her acting more like Annie viewed our relationship than I did. I mean, did that qualify as flirting?

She shifted her weight to get up and I suddenly didn't want her to leave. I didn't want to be alone. "I heard you turned forty recently," I said.

She sat back down and nodded. "Yeah. Just a number, Chief. No big deal."

"Are we friends?" I asked and felt my cheeks flushing. Those words just slipped out and I felt betrayed by them.

She got that tender look on her face again and then smiled so bright I almost had to look away. "God. I sure hope so. This town would suck without you. You make it a better place to live. For all of us."

I wanted to ask her more. To say something serious. But I didn't have it in me. "So do you," I said.

Her smile vanished and she studied my face, her eyes intense and unrelenting, but not like Annie. There was a gentleness there.

My ex-wife had been intense, sometimes I think Annie imprinted on me in terms of relationships. After high school, I picked someone very much like Annie and married her.

Lila's whole way of being was very different. I still

couldn't see her as more than a friend, but I had to wonder if I had been missing out on something.

"Okay," she said, her smile coming back. "So friends." She put her hand out and we shook hands.

Her eyes roamed around nervously again, and it was finally enough to break through my self-obsessed funk.

"Something going on, Lila?" I asked. "You know you are friends with the chief of police and aren't to be messed with."

She smiled and shook her head, the bell on her hat tinkling, but the smile wasn't quite real. "Just too many shoes dropping lately. I'm just expecting another one to come crashing down. At any moment."

"Well, I can relate to that," I said, taking a sip of the drink.

"Listen, friend Chief," she said as she got up. "I've got to work in the morning and need a couple of hours sleep. I'm over forty now, after all, and all-nighters are a thing of the past. Talk soon?"

I nodded and watched her scurry off.

I was puzzled but I was also left feeling like I usually did after an encounter with Lila Chang. Much lighter and even a little bit happy despite the disaster this day had been.

That was the last time I saw her alive.

PART 2

INVESTIGATION: CHRISTMAS DAY

SEVEN

7:12 AM CHRISTMAS MORNING. CARTER HILL.

MY OLD MAN ONCE TOLD ME THAT RESPONSIBILITY IS THE ability to respond. Which as a teenager was a big fat "duh" moment. I mean, it wasn't much of a trick, just a disassembling and reordering of the word.

I didn't have much responsibility back then. I was a teenager. The scope of things I could effectively respond to was sadly limited. Add on to that the roaring stew of hormones coursing through my veins and it's a good thing I didn't have the ability to respond to much.

When he told me, I was in the middle of a love triangle with Annie Smith having just left Frank Paulson to be with me. I was missing my best friend and obsessed with Annie.

Passion had changed us. And my father was telling me that I had a responsibility, an ability to respond to the situation and make it right. With Frank. With Annie.

But I don't think I really had the ability to respond. Sure I bore some responsibility for the situation, but because of the hormones and the aforementioned caveman biology, I couldn't break up with Annie and try to make it right with Frank.

I didn't have the ability. Not yet.

Staring at the body of Lila Chang under the tree, her blood on the white snow, I had to wonder. Was this part of another love triangle with Annie involved? She had been so obsessed with my relationship with Lila, which I didn't really understand.

And being the chief of police, I had a responsibility to find the murderer and bring them to justice. And if Annie was involved that put me in an extremely awkward situation.

But I also had a responsibility last night when I was too caught up in my own drama to really be there for Lila.

That's the thing about responsibility. The weight of it often overwhelms your very human ability to respond. At least it does for me.

I was alone with Lila. Lester was off getting the doctor. Annabelle was packing up the CSI gear. The Coconino Sheriff's Department were sending a couple of deputies out. Mary Reilly wasn't here yet. And the people that would be tearing down the tent shortly hadn't showed up.

Every time I looked at Lila's body slumped against the tree it hit me again. Like a knife to my gut.

She was dead. The cheery Christmas lights wound in the tree above her were still on. The sky was a startling bright blue. Both of those things completely incongruous given what had happened here.

"I'm sorry," I whispered to her, a cloud of condensate briefly blurring my view of her. "I failed you. I..."

I brushed at my eyes. Maybe that wasn't just condensate

blurring things up. I shivered from more than the cold that was starting to permeate me despite the CPD parka I had on.

And, yeah, I'll admit that moment was a little dramatic. But I felt responsible. I suspected that if I had been clearer yesterday, I could have done something to stop this. I wasn't a teenager. I was a middle-aged man in a position of power and responsibility. I had the ability to respond and it was my duty.

I was still standing on the road staring at Lila slumped against the tree. If you ignored the blood, it seemed like she was a tired elf who had just taken a break. Maybe enjoying the sparkling cold morning.

The weight of it was heavy. I was sorry. I had failed her. She had already paid the greatest price, but there was a price to be paid. For me. For whoever did this. For the town as a whole.

You don't see many murders in a town like Carterville. Domestic violence, unfortunately, yes. But not murders.

I had been at this enough to know I wouldn't like what was coming. Beyond wrestling with my grief and my responsibility here, I would have to pull back the curtain and find out who Lila really was.

Why would someone want to kill her?

Why was she so secretive about her past?

When did the murder happen? She left before I did, before Frank and a lot of the catering staff. Had she been killed before we all left and we all just missed it?

A breeze kicked up, bringing with it stinging needles of hard snow, and I shivered. I turned away from Lila's body. She had been so alive just a few hours ago and I was still having trouble accepting the reality. I could see her smile. Feel her small hand in mine as we shook after my awkward question about being friends. I stamped my feet and started pacing. Putting aside my part in this and focusing on my job. My duty. On my ability to respond to this crime.

I started compiling the list of suspects and it wasn't pretty.

Annie Smith.

Karen Winslow.

A mysterious person from Lila's past.

This was going to be a hell of a Christmas day.

———

"You don't want to see this," I called when I saw Patty Walsh striding towards me from the overlook. Her jaw was set and her breath was coming out in brief clouds like some kind of locomotive. It was a hell of a climb to the top of the hill, metal stairs built into the hill from Fir street that bypassed the one switchback that gets cars to the top of the hill.

I should have told her to turn back, but I couldn't. Hers was a friendly face and I needed a friendly face.

But of course she knew that.

She was wearing a long brown coat that went down to her knees and the same black slacks she wore when working at the diner. In one hand was a brown paper bag that the diner used for takeout and in the other was a thermos.

There was a moment there when I actually smiled. Because Patty was clearly coming to the rescue. I was caffeine free, hungover, and starving.

Last night when I finally went home, I had quite a few more drinks, my mind going over and over what had happened with Annie. It wasn't the kind of night that I would have been able to sleep without some help.

Now, my head felt like someone had pounded a nail into it with the twin issues of a hangover and caffeine deprivation. Not to mention anger and grief on top of it all.

But my smile was only the briefest of things. The look on Patty's face snuffed it out. Her lips were pressed together in a thin line, her cheeks red from the cold, and her eyes held a fury I didn't know she was capable of.

"Really, you don't want to see this," I said when she got close.

She nodded and kept walking until she reached me and then she shoved the thermos and bag into my hand, her eyes roaming the forest until she found Lila.

It's a small town. Everyone already knew what had happened. I had already turned away several curious residents.

"I knew something was wrong," she said, her eyes locked on the elf-costumed body.

"What… what did you feel?" I asked tentatively. Patty was my friend. Patty was my dream. I wanted to comfort her, but I had a job to do.

"She was scared," Patty said slowly, her eyes still locked on Lila's prone form. "She wanted safety. I thought it was just about her store, about the mayor and the rent. I…"

I saw the tears well up in Patty's eyes, but I took a small step back because the fury in her was palpable like a radiating heat. I suddenly understood something about her. She had quit her job, shoved her belongings in her car, and left Colorado to visit her cousin in Phoenix. She did this after what she called a "bad divorce."

Now, I had a bad divorce, believe me I know how ugly it can get, but it didn't cause me to flee and leave behind everything I knew with only the belongings I could stuff in a car.

Patty's decision to stay in Carterville was made in the moment. She just stopped for food. What if she had been running from an abusive ex-husband? This was before the meteor, so Carterville was a sleepy little town. Maybe she stayed because she was scared and didn't think her ex would ever find her here. Because she felt safe.

And now something had happened to Lila and her power had given her some warning. I wasn't the only one that felt responsible.

"Can you tell me anything more than that?" I asked gently.

She kept staring at Lila, her breath coming faster. "No, not really. I get whispers of feelings from people around me. I see images of things they desire."

I swallowed hard, imagining the images she'd seen from me.

"But there were so many people last night that I had to tune it out for the most part," she continued. "I got a drink. I was alone with Lila and I felt something despite trying to tune it all out. I asked her if she was okay. She told me about the rent and laughed it off. You know how she was."

Patty wasn't looking at Lila anymore but her green eyes were locked with mine. The fury was still there, but the tears were now flowing.

My emotions were a strange jumble. I felt oddly relieved that I wasn't the only one that felt responsible for what happened to Lila. I had a sharp realization as to how hard it can be to have a power like Patty's. And I wanted to hug Patty so bad, but it wasn't the time or the place.

"You're going to find who did this, Henry. You are going to, aren't you?" she asked. There was a desperation in her voice and it reinforced my insight about her escape to Carterville.

"Was she scared of somebody?" I asked.

She took a breath that came shuddering out. "I think so. But there was more than that. She was scared and maybe… I don't know. Hopeful. Like she was looking forward to something. I… I was drinking last night and I was trying to ignore my powers. So…" She ended in a shrug.

Her eyes roamed around and she rubbed at the tears on her cheeks. She took a deep breath and squared her shoulders. "You eat, Chief. I need to get back to the diner."

I watched Patty walk away and knew in my heart that Annie had been wrong about Lila but not about Patty.

———

THERE IS SOMETHING WONDERFUL ABOUT KNOWING EVERYONE in a little town like Carterville. Most of the time. The gossip is wicked and fast and tragedies are harder to bear.

Like this one. The people driving and walking up Carter Hill were all people I knew. All people I cared about to one degree or another. And they were people that had known and cared about Lila.

Lila was the one that died, this was over for her, but it was a long way from being over for Carterville.

In between guard duty, I scarfed the breakfast burrito and downed the coffee and started feeling more human. And on this Christmas morning, feeling more human was me feeling angrier, sadder, and a lot more scared.

"What happened, Henry?" Mary Reilly asked when she got out of Martin Lester's truck. Mary was short, all of four-foot-four, deep into her seventies and looked like the postcard-perfect grandmother you'd envision in the snow-globe-perfect Carterville.

Except Mary had a superpower. If she tells someone to do something and puts the weight of her power behind it, they will do it.

Mary is not on the payroll of the Carterville Police Department, but I kind of treat her like she is. Using her and her power when it is useful. There's a couple of reasons for this. First, her power can be extraordinarily helpful. Second, her power is extraordinarily potent and I need to keep an eye on her.

It would be easier if she just left Carterville, but that would be cruel. She has Alzheimer's but something about her power and/or Carterville counteracts it. Leaving Carterville would mean a terrible ending for her.

"I don't know yet, Mary," I said. "I don't know if you want to see this."

But Mary brushed past me, a gasp escaping her lips and then she said. "Lila! Oh my dear sweet Lord. What happened to you?"

She was about to step off the road into the snow but I took a hold of her arm. She was wearing a pink down jacket with a handmade knit hat also in pink, tufts of her short white hair sticking out. She was tiny and not that strong, so she wasn't hard to stop, but I had to be gentle.

"We haven't investigated the scene yet," I said.

She stepped back and nodded, her hazel eyes connecting with mine. "What can I do?" she asked, her chin quivering.

Annabelle Unger was rolling up in the department SUV and Martin Lester was walking over to help her unload. I nodded down the road towards the overlook and the stairs there and down the road Annabelle had just driven up. "Just keep people away. And don't use your power unless you have to."

And the truth was, she probably wouldn't have to use her power unless it was a tourist. All the locals knew not to mess with old Mary Reilly.

EIGHT

7:31 AM CHRISTMAS MORNING. CARTER HILL

We are a small department so we all wear a lot of hats. Before the meteor hit, we didn't need to use them that much. But after? Well, it's gotten a lot more interesting around here.

Annabelle has a flair for crime scene investigation. She's had some training at it, enough for little Carterville things, but she had shown an aptitude for it. I had the same training as her, but she was much better at it than I was. An eye for detail, I guess.

Her purple streaked red hair was pulled back into a ponytail and under a fuzzy red hat. She wore a blue CPD parka like Lester and me. She didn't say much, her brown eyes going wide when she saw Lila's body and her jaw setting. The sun had crested the horizon, the additional illumination making the scene all that more shocking.

While Annabelle got more gear out of the SUV, I walked over to Lester. He was standing there on the edge of the road staring at the body, his big grey mustache working so I suspected he was chewing on his lower lip. He wasn't going to be much good to me up here.

"We've got a couple of people to question," I said.

He nodded, but didn't look away, his dull blue eyes a little vacant.

"It would be better if you rounded them up and brought them to the station," I said.

He nodded again, still staring.

"I'll be down in… a half an hour or so," I said. "I'd like the first one there at nine, the second at ten."

He nodded again. "Who?" he asked.

"Annie Smith and Karen Winslow," I said, keeping my voice low. It was only Annabelle and Mary up here, but this wasn't a rumor I wanted spreading.

Lester finally looked at me, his eyes wide. "If they ask me what it's about? If they don't want to come down?" he asked.

"Tell them it's an urgent CPD matter and don't tell them anything else," I said with a sigh. "If they refuse, we'll deal with it then."

Martin nodded, his eyes going back to Lila's body. He stared for a moment, his mustache working in that chewing-your-lip kind of way. And then he nodded, shrugged, and walked away.

———

Before walking toward the body came pictures. A lot of them. And video. Then working around her body from the road all the way around, stretching the yellow crime scene tape between trees. Then slowly approaching, avoiding the tracks she had made, looking for anything unusual on the snowy ground.

In some ways it was good. Focus. Action. Doing something instead of just standing around.

It was about ten yards from the road to the tree her body was slumped under.

One set of footprints in. It looked like she walked in slowly, her pace slow and tentative, pausing once in the middle, her feet shuffling there momentarily, maybe moving to turn around, and then proceeding at a faster pace to the tree and finally turning around.

It's not clear what happened when she paused, but looking at the pattern of footprints raised the hair on the back of my neck. It looked to me like she saw something that scared her. Someone behind her. Someone stalking her.

The thought of some shadowy figure threatening Lila, chasing her into the forest, set my teeth grinding and my fists clenching. I wanted to hit something. I wanted to hurt someone. I had to stop thinking about Lila.

I mean, it was hard when her vacant eyes looked like they were staring at me. Blaming me. I started thinking of her as a Jane Doe. It was the only way I could get through those moments.

When we got close to her body, we stopped, a shuddering sigh escaping Annabelle. She may be all dyed hair, high heels, and manicured nails, but she's been with me for years and was steady as hell when she needed to be.

Maybe it was the breast cancer she survived in her thirties or the child she lost in her forties or the car accident that left her learning how to walk again in her fifties.

Annabelle has been through some shit and at times like this it showed.

"What's next?" I whispered.

"Is Doc coming?" she asked.

I nodded, trying to force my brain to accept that this was a Jane Doe. This was a sad, tragic thing, but it wasn't someone I knew. Someone I cared about. Someone I needed to avenge.

And I knew there would be a price to pay for doing this to myself. But I had to do my job.

"Well, I think we best wait for her before moving the body," Annabelle said.

I nodded and felt trapped there. The iron smell of blood was undeniable and it turned my stomach, making me wish I hadn't eaten that breakfast burrito. I turned around and saw a few folks walking up and seeing Mary Reilly there with her arms crossed promptly turning around and walking away.

Reputation is its own kind of power.

I forced myself to turn back around and look at the body. I avoided the eyes and slowly examined her. Her back was to the tree but she was slumped way down. There were some darker splotches on the tree, probably blood. She was likely standing, her back pressed to the tree, when her throat was pierced.

The tree showed the effect of her slide down it, bits of bark freshly removed. I was sure we'd find evidence on her back when we got to moving the body.

She was slumped a little to her right and her head stared back out toward the road. She had been looking at her murderer when she died.

She wasn't wearing a jacket. Which didn't make any sense. It was cold last night, and while her elf costume was more substantial than your cheap store-bought kind, it wasn't up to the cold of winter at seven thousand feet elevation.

Her hands appeared to have casually fallen onto the crusty snow, one to her left and one to her right. Her right hand seemed to have scratched the snow. It looked like a V, but I couldn't quite tell, her hand blocking part of it.

"She gave us a clue," I said, pointing it out to Annabelle.

She leaned in close and took some pictures. I just had my cell phone as a camera, but she had a nice Canon DSLR with a telephoto lens.

"A V?" she asked. "Was she trying to write a name or tell us something else?"

I shrugged.

Annabelle leaned in and took pictures of the wound. It was dark with crusted blood that had frozen, looking like a dark little void. "Where is the murder weapon?" she asked.

"I suspect powers," I said.

Annabelle looked at me, her brown eyes wide, her bright red lips moving. She blinked and looked back at the body. "Chief, I..." she began, her eyes going to the wound and then back to me again. "I need to step away from this investigation."

"What?" I asked.

"My power, Chief," she said, her eyes even wider.

"No..." I said as I began to see it. Her power was a bit like Arnold Hughes's but quirkier. She could levitate things. But they had to be small and she could only do it briefly. Could she levitate a small sharp object and do this? And that V might have been the start of an A.

She nodded grimly and swallowed.

"I've never seen you move something fast," I said.

She bit her lip and looked sheepish, the smile lines around her mouth deepening.

"Goddamnit, Annabelle," I said. I was mad because she had been holding out on me regarding her power. I was also mad because she was right. "Don't say anything else. Hand me the camera and walk back to the road and stay there."

I watched her go, my heart thumping in my head and I felt more alone than I had in a long time. Lester wasn't any good to me here, and Annabelle was now officially a suspect.

That's the problem with a murder in a town like this. The victim was my friend and there's a good chance the murderer was too.

NINE

8:03 AM CHRISTMAS MORNING.
CARTER HILL

Using Jenny Lion, the only doctor in Carterville, may seem like an odd choice in this situation. It would seem logical to get a medical examiner from Flagstaff to do the work.

But that would be ignoring Jenny's power.

Earlier I said that when the meteor struck it seemed to make people more of what they were. Like Patty being more empathetic. It wasn't always that way, but it was for Jenny Lion.

She could see things.

I can't tell you how it works because she's never been able to describe it in a way that my simple brain can understand, but when she tries—and there is a cost to her effort—she can "see" inside the body, see what MRIs have trouble seeing. Understand what is wrong.

When I heard a car on the road, I stood up, my knees

creaking, and saw Jenny Lion get out of her yellow Prius, the color much too cheerful for a day like today.

She was a short woman, and round, with kind brown eyes and a very plain face. She was in her early thirties, with her shoulder-length chestnut brown hair escaping a black knit hat. Parts of a tattoo visible on her neck.

I caught her eye and she gave me a grim nod. I carefully walked the path back. Annabelle was still there facing the desert and chewing on a fingernail.

"Thank you for coming, Doctor Lion," I said, pulling up the crime scene tape for her to duck under.

She's a bit of an enigma. A young woman that came to a small rural town right out of medical school to practice medicine the old-fashioned way. She also rides a motorcycle, loves to bungee jump, has more tattoos than you can count, and is a dedicated church goer singing in the choir. Since the meteor hit, she has a thriving practice that focuses on diagnostics, using her unique powers that only work in or near Carterville.

"Of course, Chief," she said. She leaned to the side and sucked in a breath when she saw Lila's body. "Oh, dear lord. This is…" Her eyes found mine and the compassion I saw there almost destroyed my tenuous "Jane Doe" illusion.

"I'm sorry to ask this of you," I said, "but the more data you can give me up front, the better."

She gave me a thin-lipped smile and nodded.

The cost of her using her power was fatigue and headaches. She strictly limited the use of them and generally only for paying clients that normal diagnostics weren't enough for.

I walked her back and squatted on the snow next to her as she looked the body over.

"Shit," she said, squatting down to get a closer look.

I nodded. This was personal for all of us.

"You want me to do it here?" she asked, looking up.

"If it doesn't affect the quality of the information, that would be helpful," I said. She was staring at the body, but I was studying her face. Watching her work. Watching her reactions.

Annie Smith and Karen Winslow being suspects was disturbing, but Annabelle's omission about her powers and exit from the case had spooked me. It wasn't in my nature, but for now I needed to suspect everyone and, in this moment, how the doctor reacted was important.

She took a deep breath and grabbed my arm, her grip strong and then quickly painful. Her face contorted in pain and her eyes went out of focus. I watched as those brown eyes scanned up and down the body, her grip hurting even more, sweat beading on her forehead despite the cold.

It didn't take long. A minute, maybe two. I knew she would end up with a headache, and I probably had a bruise. At one point when the doctor was looking at Lila's abdomen, she swore.

She closed her eyes, sucking in a deep breath and rocking back. She pulled on me hard and steadied herself.

"What is it?" I asked.

"She is..." she began with a gulp. "She was... she was pregnant."

———

DOCTOR LION WAS GONE. TWO COCONINO COUNTY SHERIFF'S deputies had taken over the crime scene. I had sent Annabelle home and told her not to leave town. Annie Smith was waiting in my office, but still I was up on Carter Hill looking out over the desert.

The temperature was up around thirty and that was a relief, but my face felt frozen and numb which was an odd companion to my aching heart.

Jenny Lion had confirmed the cause of death, her left carotid artery had been pierced. She also told me that there were no sizeable remnants of the murder weapon in the body and that the time of death was between 1:00 AM and 2:00 AM.

But that wasn't what kept me up there.

Lila Chang had been pregnant. She was about six weeks along. There were two deaths here, not one, and a truck load of complications.

The mysterious father was now on the suspect list.

And no one seemed to know about Lila's pregnancy. In a small town like this, that is a hard secret to keep.

A Coconino County medical examiner was on the way. Since it was Christmas Day, they would be cursing my name for a long time. I changed my mind about having Doctor Lion do it all. What she did do was valuable, but I needed outside confirmation. And a tox screen. Doctor Lion's powers don't work at that level.

"Penny for your thoughts, Chief," Mary Reilly said. She was still up here keeping the looky-loos away.

"You can go home, Mary," I said, looking down at the old woman with a smile. I'm afraid it wasn't much of a smile, but it was the best I could do. "The sheriff's deputies have got this now."

She nodded. "I'll be lucky if William hasn't opened all the presents yet. He's older than I am and still can be such a child."

"That's one of his best qualities," I said.

She nodded and looked out at the desert. The view is… I don't know how to describe it. On a cold, clear day you can see the cut of the Grand Canyon forty-five miles away. And you can see the land as the trees seem to shrink to bushes and then to shrubs and then to nothing as the browns, tans, and muted reds of the desert take over. Arizona has many views where it seems like you can see forever, but only one like this.

But today, it was lost on me. My emotions changed the experience. This view usually gives me perspective, the vastness of it putting my troubles in context, but today I was just getting madder and madder.

At myself for missing so much. At Annie for being… Annie. At the murderer for what they just did to Lila and my town.

"You want a piece of advice, Chief?" Mary asked.

I licked my lips and nodded, although it was one of the last things I wanted right then.

"It might be worth considering turning this investigation over to those fine deputies." Her voice was gentle and her words chosen carefully so that she did not engage her power.

Still it felt like a blow.

This was my town. My responsibility. Lila was my friend.

But I didn't say anything like that. "Thanks, Mary. I'll think about it. Give William my best and enjoy the rest of your Christmas."

I watched Mary slowly walk to her car, her husband William had driven up here to get her. I watched them drive off down the hill. I should have gone but still I watched and still I waited.

I knew Annie was going to be angrier the longer she waited, but that was just fine with me.

TEN

9:18 AM CHRISTMAS MORNING.
CARTERVILLE POLICE DEPARTMENT

"I hope this isn't some sick way of trying to make up with me," Annie Smith said when I walked in the Carterville Police Department. "It's Christmas morning, for God's sake."

I was back in my everyday brown cowboy hat. I wasn't sure if I was ever going to be able to wear the beautiful silver one again.

Annie was sitting on the empty desk, folders pushed aside, her arms crossed and her lips pursed into a thin line. She looked tired and her hair was pulled back into a ponytail, unusual for her. She had on her work clothes, a white dress shirt with a thin black tie and a black skirt and vest. It was Christmas morning which was a busy time at the inn.

Martin Lester was at his desk not far from Annie looking positively uncomfortable as he pretended to tap away at his computer.

"I'm afraid not," I said, keeping my tone as even as I could. "We have some questions for you regarding last night."

Emotions quickly passed over her face—surprise, concern, curiosity—and if I didn't know Annie as well as I do, I would have missed the flash of guilt. My stomach tightened.

"I need to know your whereabouts last night," I said. "You left the party around 10:30, can you tell me where you were between then and 3:00 AM."

I pulled out my little notebook and pen from my back pocket. Taking notes is a good habit to have. There's nothing wrong with my memory, but I've found that we all tend to trust our memories a lot more than we should.

Annie's face softened. "I know it wasn't a good night for us, Henry," she said, her eyes going from me to Lester. "But this is not the way for us to talk about it."

I took my parka off and hung it on a hook on the wall near the door. "This is part of a CPD investigation, Annie."

"What investigation?" she asked.

I turned and looked at her. I wanted to see her reaction. I am no empath like Patty, but I've done this job long enough to have a good idea what guilt looks like. "Lila Chang was murdered last night."

Annie twitched like I had just slapped her, her mouth opening wide and then slamming shut. Her cheeks flushed red. "You… you don't think I did it, do you?" she asked.

"What I think doesn't matter here," I said. "Given our exchange last night I have to ask you these questions."

"I'm a suspect?" she said, sliding off the desk and taking a step toward me, her voice loud.

"Yes," I said. While I had a hard time distancing from Lila when I was up on Carter Hill so that I could just do my job, I was having a much easier time treating Annie as a suspect.

This was very telling in regards to our relationship. Something broke last night and badly. It was only now becoming clear.

"Can you tell me where you were between 10:30 PM last night and 3:00 AM this morning?" I asked.

Her head swiveled and I don't know what kind of look she gave Lester, but he blanched. When she turned back to me, I thought I saw a flash of guilt again and then her face softened. "Can we go into your office, Henry?"

I shook my head. "That wouldn't be wise," I said. "Given our relationship and our recent discussion regarding the deceased, it is not a good idea for me to question you alone."

While I had no intention of doing what Mary Reilly suggested and turning this investigation over to someone else, she hadn't been wrong to say it. There was some tricky territory to navigate here.

"Does it have to be him?" she said, and I felt bad for Lester. Annie was not fond of the older man and her scorn was a well-honed instrument. "Where is Annabelle?"

"She is not available," I said. "And, no, it doesn't have to be Officer Lester. If you would like a lawyer present, I understand."

As I think back on this exchange, I think my calmness is what surprises me the most. Just over twenty-hour hours earlier I woke up in her bed and the dreaded gift was given that seemed to start all this madness. But something took over and I just did my job. I was calm on the surface. I even felt calm. But that was a lie I was telling to myself. There was a storm brewing and, in some ways, holding it off and being so calm was only going to make it worse.

"I don't need a goddamn lawyer," Annie said, her nostrils flaring and her breath coming fast. Her eyes darted around the room and then a wicked smile crossed her face. "I want Mary Reilly. Get Mary and I'll tell you exactly where I was last night."

I knew Annie and this was her fighting back. Whatever she had to tell me, I wasn't going to like it.

————

KAREN WINSLOW CAME IN FOR QUESTIONING. GIVEN THAT IT was Christmas morning, I was rather surprised. But I could see from the haunted look on her lean face that she had heard the news and she probably had a good idea why I wanted to ask her questions.

"Can I get you some coffee?" I asked from behind my desk. Annie was out in the main office, and at this point it was best that we not be too close. The looks she had been stabbing at me were meant to damage.

Karen sighed and shook her head as she sat down in the chair across from my desk. She didn't say anything, leading me to believe that unlike Annie she knew exactly what this was about and had thought it through.

She unzipped her expensive down jacket and her perfume came wafting out, stronger than usual, too strong in my tiny office. She had on a glittering green sweater that looked to me like it was expensive, but then again, my sense of fashion doesn't go much past cowboy hats.

I held up a recorder. "I'll need to tape our conversation or I can have Officer Lester come in. He's out on an errand but will be back soon."

"Tape away," she said.

And, yes, I could have offered Annie this option but

hadn't. Frankly, it hadn't occurred to me. And looking back, I think it was because I really didn't want to be in a room alone with her.

"I presume you've heard about Ms. Chang," I said.

She blinked and nodded.

I did a quick test of the recorder, making sure it was working and started it. "December 25, 2017, 9:48 AM. Interview between Henry Carter and Karen Winslow regarding the murder of Lila Chang this morning between 1:00 and 2:00 AM. Please state your name for the record."

Karen leaned forward, her voice a bit louder than it needed to be. "Karen Ann Winslow, mayor of Carterville."

I suppressed a smile. I didn't ask her to state her occupation. Karen was fighting this as vigorously as Annie, just in a different way.

"You attended the Carterville Silver Ball last night, is that correct?" I asked.

She nodded. "Yes. Along with you and most of the town."

"What time did you leave?" I asked.

She shrugged. "About 9:15 PM, as I recall. Ken was tired and wanted to get back to the ranch."

"Did you spend the night at the ranch?" I asked.

She shook her head. "No. I had some paperwork to attend to and stayed at the office last night. Ken dropped me off on his way home."

The Winslows have an apartment above some of the shops on the Circle. It's more than just an office. It has workspaces, but it's also a living space, one of the nicest in towns.

"What time did you leave?" I asked.

"I was about to leave a little after 7:30 AM when Officer

Lester called," she said. "I didn't leave until it was time for this interview."

"When did you arrive at the apartment last night?" I asked.

She shrugged. "Around 9:30."

"Can anyone corroborate that you were there?" I asked.

She shook her head. "Except for Ken dropping me off, I was alone."

I stared into her hazel eyes and wished we were having a real conversation here. She wasn't really a practicing lawyer anymore, but all that training showed. She wasn't going to give me anything I didn't ask for.

Her being a suspect and not having an alibi was more than a little awkward. With her being the mayor and me being the chief of police. With her being a Winslow and me being a Carter.

Part of me wanted it to be her. Not that Lila dying could ever be acceptable, but getting rid of Karen would be good for this town.

"Can you explain your plans for the Carterville Brewery to me?" I asked, being careful to keep my tone even.

A brief flicker of surprise passed over her face. She didn't think I knew, but she recovered quickly. "How does that relate to this investigation?"

"Ms. Chang felt you were trying to force her out of her shop so you could use it for the brewery," I said.

Her jaw clenched briefly and her eyes narrowed. Just a small flash of the anger that I am sure was roiling below the surface. She must have known she was a suspect, but I don't think she had fully grasped it until then. And she was mad about it.

She smiled, it was a stiff, unconvincing thing, and swallowed. "'Force' is a strong word," she said. "But yes, I was interested in terminating her lease early."

"So you raised her rent three times this year in an attempt to do that?" I asked.

She leaned back and studied me. Carterville may be a small town, but that doesn't mean she wasn't a skilled politician. She knew me and she knew me well and wasn't above pushing my buttons.

"Were you and Lila close?" she asked.

Her using Lila's first name made me want to hurt her. I tried to keep my face neutral, but I'm sure some of that emotion leaked out. "Please answer my question," I said.

"Can you repeat the question?" she asked, clearly stalling.

"Ms. Chang," I began, emphasizing the name the way I wanted her to say it, "told me you raised her rent three times this year. Was this an attempt to force her out so you could use the space for your own business?"

She blinked and nodded minutely.

"Can you please speak your answer for the record," I said.

"Yes," she said. "Lila didn't want to move her shop so I used the levers legally available to me to encourage her to do so."

"Levers?" I asked.

She sighed and her shoulders slumped. Maybe the lawyer in her was telling her that this was a valid line of questioning and she had to answer.

"Levers," she said, nodding again. "I raised her rent and I offered her another space for her business at a lower cost."

"But she refused?" I asked.

"Yes. Lila didn't want to leave the Circle," she said.

Not all thriving businesses were on the Circle, but most of them were, or just above or just below it.

"And the antique shop next door owned by Emily Underwood," I said. "You've been using 'levers' there as well?"

"It's just business," Karen said, leaning forward. "Surely you understand that, Henry. It was nothing personal, I just need the space."

I met her stare and held it. In some cases all those clichés about a guilty person betraying themselves are true, but often they are not. The evidence is what tells the story, regardless of what your gut says.

And my gut wasn't saying that Karen was guilty, but it was hoping that she was.

Besides, I wouldn't expect Mayor Karen Winslow to say anything that she didn't want me to know.

"Did you kill Lila Chang?" I asked.

She kept staring right at me. "No."

"Do you know who killed Lila Chang?" I asked.

"No."

"Did you play any role in the murder of Lila Chang?"

She paused, and I could see her fighting to keep the anger in. Good. I was doing the same.

"No," she said, a little louder this time.

My phone chimed and I looked down. It was a text from Lester. Mary Reilly was here.

And then it hit me. I knew why Annie had asked for Mary, and I just wanted to throw up. But it was a useful thought, one that I could use.

"Thank you for answering my questions," I said with the best smile I could manage.

"Are we done?" she asked.

I nodded and turned off the recorder.

As Karen got up, I said, "Mary Reilly is here. I was

wondering whether you'd be willing to answer those last three questions under her influence."

She blinked and stared at me, her brow furrowing and then she smiled. "No, I would not be willing to subject myself to your questions under Mary Reilly's influence," she said. "I have a feeling those questions would escape the boundaries of this investigation."

I just stared at her. Of course she didn't trust me. I sure as hell didn't trust her.

"And I trust that you will be sensitive to the season and the economic realities of Carterville and be discrete with your investigation," she said.

In other words, don't scare the tourists. I only ground my teeth together briefly before answering. "You can trust that I will do my job and bring the killer to justice."

She zipped up her coat and smiled wider. "Merry Christmas, Henry. Looks like it's going to be a memorable one for you."

She was at the door, about to open it, when I said, "One last thing. Don't leave town."

Karen whipped around, surprise on her face.

I enjoyed her surprise, but realized my request could use some tempering. "I'm sure you'll want to be kept informed of developments. And I might have a few more questions for you."

She frowned but nodded and left before I could say anything else.

ELEVEN

ANNIE AND I WERE THROUGH. DONE. FOR GOOD THIS TIME. I knew it the moment I saw her face as she and Mary Reilly walked in my office.

It wasn't an unusual look of her lovely face, which was distant and businesslike, it was just an unusual look for her to give me. Annie was lovely, but she was a lot less lovely today than she was a couple of days ago. Her features hadn't changed, I had. Or our relationship had. So my perception of her had.

That "beauty lies in the eyes of the beholder" saying is certainly rooted in the truth. When things were good with Annie there was no one more beautiful to me. Now... well, with the bland expression she was showing me, she wasn't nearly as beautiful anymore.

And I'm sure I looked older, paunchier, and more worn out to her today than I had a few days ago.

"Thank you for waiting, Annie," I said, standing up as the

two women walked in. Lester brought in an extra chair and then left, closing the door behind him. I saw a flash of pity and relief on his face as he escaped.

With three people in my closet of an office, it was officially crowded.

"I think you should hold off on thanking me, Henry," Annie said with a wry smile.

"And my apologies to William," I said to Mary. "Did he get to open his presents yet?"

Mary nodded and smiled. "That he did." The smile evaporated from her face as her hazel eyes went to Annie and then back to me. "He sends his love and said to tell you to 'get the bastard.'"

"Please sit," I said, gesturing to the two chairs.

Mary sat with a sigh, and Annie sat stiffly on the edge of her chair.

I opened my mouth to start the questions when Annie held up her hand. It was a gesture I had seen her use pretty often on her employees, but it wasn't one she used on me very much. I felt my cheeks flush.

"Mary," she said. "Will you do it? Please."

The old woman nodded and took a deep breath, her eyes locked with Annie's. "You will answer Chief Carter's questions honestly and completely regarding last night."

It was just one sentence, a single phrase, and yet it felt to me like the air was crackling. Mary's voice got deeper and gravelly. Annie's cheek twitched like she had been slapped. And I was once again reminded why I kept Mary so close. Her power was serious and formidable and I never wanted to feel it directed at me.

"Shall we begin?" I asked.

Annie gave me a grim smile. "Please. It is a busy day at the inn and I should be there."

As of yesterday, her plans were to be with me today. My stomach tightened and I gripped the arm of my chair. This was going to be a bumpy ride.

"Where were you between 10:30 PM last night when you left the Silver Ball and 2:00 AM this morning?"

"I was with Arnold Hughes," she said, the expression on her face hard to read. The words came out slowly and I saw a widening of her eyes and a flash of surprise, but then her face hardened and she took a deep breath. "I was mad at you, Henry. You and your goddamn Carterville haram, so I let him take me to his house and I let him take me to bed."

My heart thumped loudly in my ear and my cheeks felt like they were on fire. This was why she wanted Mary. She wanted her alibi to be unimpeachable. This was Annie's way of breaking up with me once and for all.

The older woman mumbled under her breath and looked away. Annie hadn't told her the full extent of what was going to come out.

"And it was quite enjoyable," she added. "Both times. Youthful vigor, you know."

It was like time slowed down as my brain rather cruelly played images of Annie with the younger, handsomer, fitter man. My jaw moved, but I couldn't find words. My heart thumped loudly and then fluttered and skipped a beat... or ten. I felt sweat beading at my forehead and the mothball old lady smell of Mary made me want to puke.

"Any other questions, Henry?" Annie asked, shifting her weight forward to get up.

"Yes," I managed to say, the word coming out like a weak bark.

I took a deep breath and looked down at my notes. The words didn't make any sense, not even the letters. They were chicken-scratch scribbles, the doodles of a crazy man. But I didn't need my notes. I was just buying time.

"Do you…" I began and swallowed hard. "Do you know anyone that would have wanted to harm Lila Chang?" I felt sweat trickle down my lower back and it felt like I had just run a race.

Annie paused, blinking, like she had just remembered what this was about. That someone had died. That a friend of ours had been murdered.

She looked down at her hands.

"No. Everyone loved Lila," she said. "But…"

"But what?" I asked, still staring at my notes.

Annie was silent so I finally looked up. She looked scared. "I've heard things. Rumors really. She used to be married. To a very bad man."

I nodded for her to continue.

"She changed her name when she moved here," Annie said. "She didn't like to be photographed. Maybe her past caught up with her."

And then something occurred to me. That question wasn't about last night. Annie could have lied. I needed to ask her more direct questions about last night.

Looking back, the chain of thought still makes sense, but I was hurting. While I had feared Annie's confession about last night, I had hoped it wasn't true. Hope was gone and I was left with the grief of our broken relationship.

So I asked her the same questions I had asked Karen Winslow.

"Did you kill Lila Chang?" I asked.

Annie blinked as if confused and then said, "No! I was with Arnie all night."

I swallowed hard and continued. "Do you know who killed Lila Chang?"

Her cheeks flushed and her eyes flashed dangerously. "No. Of course not."

"Did you play any role in the murder of Lila Chang?" I asked, regretting each word as it came out.

Annie surged to her feet. "No!" she shouted. "I didn't kill your girlfriend in waiting, but I certainly can't say that I'm sorry she's gone."

She stormed out of the office and I was left there with a wide-eyed Mary Reilly staring at me.

TWELVE

10:42 AM CHRISTMAS MORNING.
CARTER HILL

I was back at the crime scene. Lila's body was gone and all that was left was the blood-soaked snow that she had died in, a dark stain on the pristine white.

The temperature was just above freezing. Cold but bearable, and I heard the distant sound of Christmas carols floating up from the speakers on Main Street. The sound of banging and the garbled sounds of workers came from the tent site as the crew broke it down.

Earlier I described Carterville as such a perfect little town for Christmas that it looked like a snow globe. Now that snow globe had a horrible stain at the top, making it clear that the snow globe impression we all work so hard to present was just an illusion.

The autopsy was several days off and I felt defeated. Like I should go home and get good and drunk for Christmas. Do like the mayor had suggested and go easy, let the tourists leave before pursuing it further.

Martin Lester and the two Coconino County sheriff's deputies were watching from the road. They needed me to tell them what to do.

Annie Smith was no longer on the suspect list.

Karen Winslow was, but I didn't think she did it. She had killer instincts as a businesswoman, but I didn't think she was an actual killer. Her performance while I questioned her was done for a reason. She didn't want an alibi. I suspected she wanted me to come after her, some step in a bizarre plan to get rid of me and solidify her hold on the town.

I still needed to question Annabelle, but I didn't think she had done it either. Her recusal from the case was just the right thing to do.

That left the theoretical ex-husband that Annie had mentioned or the father of her child. Lila was nervous last night, but I had nothing more than that to support the idea that either one of them was the culprit.

There were no cameras up here, and if a local had seen something last night, they would probably have come forth by now. All we had was the mysterious 911 call. It wasn't even noon yet and the case had already gone cold.

I squatted down. Without Lila's body there, I could see the scratch she made in the snow. It was definitely a V, the lines about two inches long, a little unsteady but clear. Not something she could have done by accident. At the upper right edge of the V it looked like she began to draw down again. Maybe she was just passing out. Maybe she was trying to draw another letter. Maybe it wasn't a letter but something completely different.

I studied the ground for other clues but found nothing. I

stood up, my knees creaking loudly, and examined the tree. Just some blood and flecked off bark.

I looked toward the back of Carter Hill. I couldn't see it, but the old Carter Mine was back there. Where the meteor hit and burrowed under us, giving us these powers.

Who besides Annabelle could have caused that wound, that piercing of the neck and the carotid artery without leaving a trace of evidence? If powers were involved then the crazy ex-husband theory didn't make sense.

And what about her pregnancy? The secret she had kept in a town full of wagging tongues and virulent gossip. My money was on the father of her child being the murderer. Whoever that was.

I realized I was gritting my teeth. Again. I took a deep breath and tried to relax my jaw. To hell with Karen Winslow and not scaring off the tourists. Lila was murdered along with her unborn child.

To hell with Annie Smith. We were broken up for good this time, and while it hurt, I felt some relief. Trying to please that woman for more than a moment here and there had been pretty much impossible.

And to hell with whoever did this. I was going to find them and I was going to lock them up.

"We need to canvas the neighborhood," I shouted as I carefully walked back to the road and ducked under the yellow crime scene tape. "It's Christmas morning and I'll understand if you want to go be with your families, but I need someone to stay up here. Church will be starting soon, and I need the rest of you to knock on doors with me."

I paused. It wasn't an inspiring speech or anything. Martin

Lester stood there, his hands shoved in his blue parka. The two deputies, one a young man, the other a young woman, hadn't been long on the job and they looked a little squeamish. I didn't know them. Maybe they had never been to Carterville but had heard a lot of stories. And having seen the bloody dead body of an elf on Christmas morning, they believed them all.

"Well?" I asked.

The woman, her name badge said Ortega, stepped forward. She was short and built like a fireplug with brown eyes, light brown skin, and dark hair braided in the back. She was young, and from my middle-aged perspective she could be sixteen or she could be twenty-six. I couldn't really tell the difference.

"I'm all in, Boss," she said with a shy smile. "Whatever you need."

———

To their credit, both deputies stayed. The young man guarding the crime scene and Ortega heading down the stairs from the overlook to Fir Street, the uppermost residential street on Carter Hill, to pound on doors, disturb people on Christmas, and see if they had seen or heard anything early this morning.

I was on the phone doing the kind of thing Annabelle would have normally done. Working on getting phone and bank records for Lila.

Martin Lester was standing next to me, kicking at the road still sloppy with some dirty slush on the edge, his hands shoved into his pockets.

"Shouldn't you be banging on doors, Martin?" I asked when I got off the phone.

He looked up at me, his brow furrowed and his big mustache wagging like he was trying to say something. He shrugged. "Just somethin' I should say."

I looked at him closely. His eyes wouldn't meet mine. Earlier I had just thought he was squeamish because he'd only been a cop in Carterville and he knew the victim. But now, something was clearly going on.

"Well, spit it out then, Officer," I said, my words coming out harsher than I would have liked.

He flinched like I had slapped him. "Annabelle's not here because of her power, right?" he asked.

I nodded. "Yes. She recused herself."

"Well, I guess I better do the same," he said.

My teeth set to grinding and it took an effort of will to stop. Not that I could relax my jaw at this point. My hangover and low-sleep headache was blossoming into a driving pain behind my left eye.

"Explain," I said.

"I suspect you know that Lila was pregnant with Doc Lion up here earlier," he said, his words coming out slowly.

I blinked and did my best to hide my surprise. "I do."

His tired blue eyes met mine briefly before they went back to studying the dirty snow he was kicking. "Well... I..."

"Just spit it out," I said.

"I... I'm the father," he said, shoving his hands deeper into his pockets.

We didn't stay on Carter Hill after Martin Lester's confession. I told him to shut up. Three times. He had started talking about it and now he couldn't keep it in. We got in the CPD SUV and headed back to the office.

Even then, he kept trying to talk and I kept telling him to shut up. I wasn't nice about it. I was furious. That he took this long to tell me. That there was so much going on right under my nose in my town that I didn't know about. That Lila was dead and the two people I worked with every day could be a part of it.

I marched him into my office, sat down, and started the recorder. "December 25, 2017, 11:21 AM. Interview between Henry Carter and Martin Lester regarding the murder of Lila Chang this morning between 1:00 and 2:00 AM. Please state your name for the record."

It felt silly doing this with one of my officers, but the limb

I was out on here was getting weaker and weaker. Both of my employees had to recuse themselves. This wasn't good.

"Martin Lester," he said, blinking way too much.

"What do you know about the murder of Lila Chang?" I asked.

He shrugged. "I don't know nothin' about that," he said.

My jaw clenched again. I could see myself in the near future spending a lot of time in a dental chair because of this case. "Tell me what you know about Ms. Chang's pregnancy."

His mustache wagged in that particular way and I knew that he was chewing on his lip again. Now that the recorder was going, he was having trouble talking.

My mouth was dry and I thought I smelled blood, like the scent had clung to me up at the crime scene. I wanted a shower and a drink so bad. I didn't want to be watching my friend struggle in front of me. Watching the fear and guilt flash across his face.

He was about to tell me about things I didn't know about Lila. Things I probably didn't want to know.

Lester cleared his throat and coughed, his dull blue eyes studying the mess of files and other paperwork covering my beat-up metal desk.

I was about to say something when he finally found the words.

"She had just lost a child when she came here," he said slowly. "Her husband had… he had…"

"Domestic violence?" I asked, trying to find words that weren't overly charged.

He nodded, his eyes briefly meeting mine. Something was haunting him. "I got hooked on her espresso," he said with a weak shrug. "We became friends. Real slow at first, she was so guarded, but after a few years she started to open up. We both loved Star Wars and we both have celiac disease."

He chuckled and smiled, the memory of bonding with her obviously a good one. "Weird thing to bond over," he continued. "I mean, having a bad gut isn't exactly proper conversation, but you know she always had gluten-free treats at her shop."

I personally like gluten and hadn't really noticed.

He shrugged again. "After a couple of years here, Lila believed she had gotten away, that she was free." He picked up a pen off my desk and started clicking it, the sharp sound annoying the hell out of me, but I let it be.

"She changed her name, you know," he said as he clicked. "Did everything she could to hide from him, but have a life, you know."

I hadn't known she changed her name until today, but it didn't surprise me. It was obvious she was escaping to Carterville. Before the meteor hit, a lot of people did that. I mean, it's a beautiful place which makes it attractive, but mostly because it's such a small town and a ways away from anywhere.

His pale blue eyes finally met mine. "She wanted to have a baby," he said, shrugging once again as if that simple gesture could explain the complexity of what was going on. "With her big four-oh comin', she figured she was out of time. She asked me. I obliged her."

My head spun. Martin Lester had never been married and I had never known him to have a girlfriend. I was quite sure he was gay.

He must have seen the questions written on my face.

"Lila's first marriage was kind of arranged," he said. "She

didn't want to be married because she didn't like men, you know."

I nodded, more for him to continue than out of understanding.

"That there will make a marriage difficult," he said. "But she desperately wanted a child and she couldn't afford that fancy invitro stuff. And we were friends. And she knew that I... well, that I wouldn't be like her ex-husband, so..."

"So you helped her get pregnant," I offered.

"Yeah," he said and shrugged again. "Lila said I would be the baby's uncle. That I could kinda be there for him... or for her. It wouldn't be legal or anything, she doesn't trust anyone enough for that, but I could be part of their lives."

I leaned forward and took a deep breath. This was bad. Worse than I had thought. "I am so sorry, Martin," I said. "This must be so very hard for you."

He nodded, and when his eyes met mine, I saw a fury there that I had never seen before. He was always a steady, quiet man, which was one of the things that made him good in his role here. I leaned back, my old office chair creaking, but held his gaze.

"I want to help," he said. "I want to make sure we find who did this." The slight curl of his lip made it clear what he would do when he found the person responsible. Or what he wanted to do. It was the same thing I wanted to do, so I could relate, but his loss was on a different level than mine.

He had lost a close friend, a child, and a future.

FOURTEEN

ANNABELLE UNGER USED TO SMOKE, A LOT. SHE QUIT A FEW years back in her early fifties, but you can see it in her face, in the deep lines that decorated it. She liked the sun, too which added to the effect. She had a weathered look that always reminded me of the desert.

Her house was on Aspen Street, on the lower parts of Carter Hill. The view out her living room window was all trees, not the spectacular vistas you get farther up the hill.

The house was neat and busy. Lots of art on the walls, mostly landscape photos she had taken around here—she had a great eye. The couch and chairs were covered in hand-crocheted blankets (or hand knit, I don't know the difference), the hardwood of her living room was covered in a red and black oriental rug, and the small woodstove in the corner popped and emitted a comforting orange glow through its glass door.

I sipped the coffee she had brought me and stared into her brown eyes. I was on the couch and she was in a chair to my left, the recorder between us on the coffee table but off.

I had just told her about Lester and the baby. She was a suspect, so I shouldn't have, but I had to talk to someone.

"Where is he now?" she asked gently, her southern drawl soothing to my frayed nerves.

I nodded toward her front door. "Out in the car. I don't think it's safe to let him loose right now, he might…" I ended in a shrug just like Lester had been doing so much.

She took a deep breath and let it out slowly. "This here is a real problem we got, Chief."

I nodded to the recorder. "I have to interview you."

"I know. You gotta do whatcha gotta do."

I wanted to just have a conversation with my friend. We had just lost someone and one of our own had just suffered a terrible loss. But now wasn't the time.

Well, not quite the time. I sipped the coffee and stared out the window at the big junipers in Annabelle's yard. There was a swing set that saw use when her daughter and grandchildren came to visit.

She had asked for Christmas off so she could go back to Georgia, but with the Winterfest, I needed her.

We sat there in uncomfortable silence. This wasn't us. She was always someone I could bounce things off of, talk through a problem, spitball ideas. She was the mother of our humble office and it just felt wrong that it was like this.

It seemed like this morning had quickly eroded my reality. Lila was dead. Annie and I were finished. Annabelle had to recuse herself from the investigation. And Lester had such a loss that I had to keep an eye on him so he didn't do something stupid.

What the hell could be next?

I nodded, more at my thoughts than anything else. The job had to be done, and it's the job—whatever our job may be—that calls us to be more and do more than we think we can.

I clicked on the recorder, did a quick test, and with a sigh turned it on and started the interview. I had my little notepad and pen out and noted the time and place.

"December 25, 2017, 11:58 AM. Interview between Henry Carter and Annabelle Unger regarding the murder of Lila Chang this morning between 1:00 and 2:00 AM. Please state your name for the record."

Annabelle answered my question, and of the interviews I had done, she was the only one that wasn't fighting me or fighting her demons.

She had no alibi, but she had means.

She had no idea that Lila Chang was pregnant.

She hadn't been aware of the Carterville Brewery and the changes Karen Winslow was trying to make to the Circle.

After I clicked off the recorder, I handed her my pen and said, "Show me."

Her brow furrowed, her wrinkled skin making a show of it, and then her eyes narrowed and she nodded.

It was a cheap pen, and with a start I noticed the gold lettering on the black plastic that read "The Carterville Inn." It was a small thing, but it felt like a punch in the gut. I must have casually picked it up before Annie gave me that damn hat and my whole world changed.

Annabelle popped the cap off and she held it on her palm

and took a deep breath. The pen slowly rose in the air and hovered about an inch above Annabelle's palm. Her eyes were unfocused and her face relaxed, making her look ten years younger.

The pen hovered there and then it darted off and hit the wall of her living room with a soft thunk, the tip buried in the sheetrock. It stayed there for a moment before falling and clattering on to her hardwood floor.

Her powers fit the crime. With a sharper object and a good aim she could have done it and then used her telekinesis to return the murder weapon to her.

"Why?" I asked. This was Annabelle, I didn't need to spell my question out, tell her I wanted to know why she had developed the skill.

She shrugged, a shy smile on her face. "Half boredom, half thinking that skill might come in handy someday."

"Handy?" I asked.

She nodded. "Yeah, Chief. Handy. Carterville ain't the sleepy little town it once was."

I nodded back. Rarely had a thing more true been said.

I stared out the window, wishing I had a solution to this issue. I needed Annabelle and Lester to work this case with me. I couldn't do this on my own.

"I've got too much to do on this one," I said, the thought escaping me. "I wish you could help."

She gave me a compassionate smile and I had to look away. I couldn't feel what I was feeling right now. I couldn't be vulnerable. I had to do my job. But how was I going to do that with Annabelle out of commission and with me having to keep an eye on Lester the whole time?

"Me too," she said.

Silence descended and I took a sip of the coffee which had gone cold. I put it down. There's little better in this world than hot coffee and not much worse than cold.

"Can I make you a sandwich, Chief?" she asked. "You gotta eat."

I nodded absently and flipped back through my notes. Not that I thought there was anything there, but for something to do.

This case didn't feel like one of those TV shows where all the clues, quite conveniently, present themselves to the detective. Where there is one small thing that is out of place, that if you just notice it, then the picture comes into startling focus.

I mean, for one thing, I was a small-town cop. Mysteries had become a much bigger part of my life since the meteor, but it wasn't like it was the only thing I did and I had an insane amount of practice at it.

And it wasn't like this was a simple thing. Some crime committed in an isolated house on a stormy night where you know the culprit had to be one of the people there.

It could have been Lila's ex who was long gone.

It could have been some random weirdo tourist here for Winterfest that had an elf fetish.

It could have been almost anyone, including Annabelle Unger or Martin Lester despite my "gut" telling me it wasn't.

Guts can be just as stupid as our brains sometimes.

And I wasn't some dispassionate, uninvolved investigator like in one of those shows. I was in the middle of it. The murder had an effect on me, and finding who did it would likely have a huge effect on me.

This was no simple case and I knew I wouldn't walk away unscathed.

———

THE SANDWICH ANNABELLE HAD MADE WAS DONE AND I WAS stalling. She had just put another log in the woodstove, the color coming from the glass door more yellow than orange. Annabelle sat staring at it.

It was Christmas. I could let it go for the day. Go home and call my son. Or drive to Flagstaff and see my sister and niece. No one would think less of me.

Well… I would.

And this murder, this mystery was a wound for our little town, and that I could not abide. This wound could not start to heal until there was some justice. But still I sat.

Annabelle sucked in a breath and sat up straight, her brown eyes bright. "I got it, Chief!"

"What?" I asked, my heart starting to thump. "You know who did it?"

Yeah. Right. I too had watched too many of those murder mystery shows where the conclusion struck like a bolt of lightning.

"No," she said, nodding towards the front of the house. "I know what to do about Martin."

I felt a stab of guilt. I had been in here drinking coffee and eating while he was out in the cold car. "What?" I asked.

"Leave him with me," she said with a sly smile. "Put us to work. We'll stay here and keep an eye on each other. I'll write ya good notes about every last thing we do. Any phone conversation will be on speaker so both of us can hear."

I blinked, my mind catching up. It was the buddy system. I couldn't quite trust either one of them, but together…

"You are brilliant, Annabelle," I said.

"I am, ain't I?" she said with a big smile. "You can't trust Martin and you can't trust me, not completely, but I think you can trust that the murder wasn't a conspiracy between the two of us."

I just blinked. That was what I had been thinking, but hearing it said out loud was chilling. I thought about it. If it was a conspiracy between the two of them, if both of the people I worked with were murderers, were that kind of people and I had never seen it, I might as well trust them because I didn't deserve this badge or this job.

"You *can* trust the two of us, can't ya?" Annabelle asked.

I nodded and smiled. "I can trust you, Annabelle. That much I am sure of. And I know I can't trust Lester out there alone."

She nodded, but wasn't smiling this time. This wasn't going to be a walk in the park for her dealing with the very upset Martin Lester.

"I'll want an hourly check in, by voice," I said. "And radio if you find anything worthwhile."

"Absolutely," she said. "Do we have Lila's phone records yet?"

I shook my head. "Not yet. I started the ball rolling but would love to hand it off." I dug into my pocket and pulled out her phone. I had already dusted it for prints up at the crime scene. I put it down on the coffee table. "Don't suppose you are good at cracking passwords?"

One eyebrow raised.

"Not exactly procedure, Henry," she said.

I shrugged. "Desperate times and all..."

Annabelle nodded, got a yellow pad of paper, and started writing notes. I felt a wave of relief to have her back on the team. And then I felt guilty about feeling any kind of relief at all. And then I shook it off, went out and got Officer Lester, and we got to work.

FIFTEEN

12:46 PM CHRISTMAS DAY. HUGHES RESIDENCE

I couldn't have told you what I was feeling as I walked up to the door of Arnold Hughes's house. I felt like my emotions had been on the tumble dry setting for over twenty-four hours.

I didn't feel so alone with Lester and Annabelle working the case, but otherwise I felt beaten and bruised and battered.

By Lila Chang's murder. By Annie's spectacularly brutal breakup. By Martin Lester's secret baby with Lila. By this being Christmas and me being out here investigating the murder of my friend.

There were plenty of people for me to go talk to, but this one I needed to get over with.

I know that Annie had been under the influence of Mary Reilly's power when I interviewed her, but her alibi had to be confirmed. And a phone call would have been fine, and this could have waited, but I needed to look him in the eye. I needed to confront him, do something to put this Annie thing behind me before I could keep going.

Still I hesitated at his door. His house was a two-story red brick building from the thirties with a white picket fence. It had been lovingly restored and was meticulously maintained. I wanted to hate him, but I couldn't hate him for that. The meteor and the powers it bestowed us brought tourists, and the infusion of funds has made the town a lot more presentable.

My mind kept going back to the V that Lila drew in the snow with her last moments. She did that for me. She knew I would be the one to investigate. Maybe we weren't full-on friends, like her and Lester had been, but she must have known that I was fond of her. That I would take this seriously. That I would do whatever it took to make sure justice was done.

But a V?

It could be an "A" for Annie Smith. Or part of a "W" for Karen Winslow. Or an "M" for Martin Lester. Not that I could fathom that any of them did it. Not that I could—

"Oh," Arnold Hughes said, interrupting my thought. The white door to his red brick house opening.

My heart thumped in the beginnings of embarrassment until I saw a suitcase in the tiled entryway behind him. "Where's Annie?" I asked.

His brow furrowed and then his pale blue eyes showed amusement. "Sorry, Henry. She's not here. No idea where she is, actually. Now if you'll excuse me, I've got to get going."

The world shifts on us all the time. We think we understand this life we are living and then it changes. Dramatically, often, and sometimes just enough to cause your brain to stutter.

When reality isn't what you thought, it can take a moment.

That had been happening to me way too much lately, and seeing Arnold with a suitcase and without Annie was a small change, but I had had so many, my brain had trouble processing it.

It was Christmas Day. I expected to find Annie and Arnie curled up by a fire laughing about her former older, fatter boyfriend. Me.

Yeah, I know. A little bit silly. But that jealous beast lives in all of us, and while I hadn't let it out to play, it was still there.

"Is there something wrong with you, Henry?" he asked. "Do I need to call 911?"

The subtle amusement and superiority in his tone snapped me out of it and I felt a flash of embarrassment that was quickly subsumed by anger. Arnold had been waiting in the wings, ready to swoop in and take Annie, and he didn't even have the decency to spend Christmas with her?

"No," I said. "But you need to answer a few questions for me."

"Sorry, Henry," he said, taking a half step out the door. "I don't have the time."

I didn't budge. He was taller, fitter, and probably stronger than I was, but he would have had to get physical with me to get out the door.

"You can answer my questions, here and now," I said. "Or you can come down to the station with me."

That got his attention. He backed up a step, blinking. "Is this about that poor girl?" he asked.

I wanted to say something about his usage of "poor girl," but didn't have the time.

I pulled my recorder out of my jacket pocket and clicked it on. "December 25, 2017, 12:51 PM. Interview between Henry Carter and Arnold Hughes regarding the murder of Lila Chang this morning between 1:00 and 2:00 AM. Please state your name for the record."

He just stood there blinking. "What's going on Henry? Are you…? Am I…?"

I was starting to enjoy this. "Please state your name for the record."

He looked around, his eyes looking up and down the street. There were Christmas lights on and decorated trees visible in some windows. It looked like the snow globe perfect view of Carterville.

"Maybe we should go inside," he said.

I gave him a purse-lipped smile and followed him inside.

When the door was closed, he said, "I gotta tell you, I feel a little ambushed here." He brushed at his bangs, his baby face looking a bit haggard.

I didn't say anything.

"You know," he said. "I have an alibi. I was with…" His eyes widened as if he was finally realizing who I was and how very awkward this conversation should be.

I held out my recorder. "Please state your name for the record."

He swallowed hard. "Ummm… Arnie Hughes."

I was there just to corroborate Annie's alibi, but seeing him squirm was way too satisfying. "You were seen leaving the Silver Ball last night at about 10:30 PM," I said. "Can you account for your whereabouts between then and 3:00 AM?"

His brow furrowed again, which made him look more his age, and that made me feel a little bit better. "I was... you know... We were here."

I didn't say anything, just held the recorder closer.

He swallowed again. "I was with Annie Smith last night," he said, looking slightly surprised as if the words just slipped out.

"Until what time?" I asked, the unbidden images of Annie and Arnie flashing through my head destroying any fun I was having. Images of them floating in the air together naked.

He shrugged. "I don't know. She was gone when I woke up."

"What time did you go to sleep?" I asked.

He shrugged. "After midnight. But I was tossing and turning, too much food, I think. So, Annie... she... you know."

I nodded to the recorder. "Please state it clearly for the record."

"She knocked me out," he said. "With her powers. I slept like a baby."

My heart started thumping hard. "What time was that?" I asked.

"She told me to go to the bathroom first," he said. "That it would be that deep of a sleep and I didn't want to risk an accident. Did this freaky little laugh. I remember looking at the clock. It was 12:49."

A cold sweat beaded on my forehead. Annie didn't have an alibi. And I believed him because Annie had told me that thing about the bathroom before, and I had heard that laugh.

I ran through her interview in my mind. The words Mary had used on her and her power. The answers she had given.

There didn't seem to be any wiggle room, but she had left this very important detail out.

"Can I go now?" he asked.

"No," I said, clicking off the recorder.

"No?" he shot back, his face looking like I had just told him he was a bad boy and had to go to bed without dinner. "What do you mean, 'no'?"

I smiled, hoping it was half as sharp as the smiles Annie was capable of. "I mean, I'm investigating a murder and I might have more questions for you soon. Sorry if that is an inconvenience."

He bit his lip, narrowed his eyes, and slowly shook his head. "This is about Annie, isn't it? You are trying to punish me."

I didn't answer. He might have been right. In that moment, I couldn't have told you.

"You needn't worry," he said. "She's still stuck on you and I'm not fool enough to be in a real relationship with that woman. Fun for a night, but longer than that…"

He trailed off with a practiced sneer and I wanted to smash his face and make it less youthful looking.

I turned, my fists clenched. "Leave town and I'll track you down and arrest you," I said.

"On what grounds?" he asked.

I paused, my back to him. "Does it matter, Arnie? I don't think being hauled into the station in regards to a murder investigation will be good for your business."

"You'll be hearing from my lawyer," he yelled after me.

———

I WAS IN THE CPD SUV AND ARNOLD HUGHES WAS STARING AT me from his door, his arms crossed. I wanted to flip him off and roar away with screeching tires. I had once done that to Frank Paulson when we were teenagers and fighting over Annie Smith.

But I wasn't a teenager anymore.

I just stared at him. Because I wanted him to be uncomfortable. Because of how he was treating Annie. For how he came between us.

And I wanted him to be the murderer.

Okay, that sounds weird. I hated that Lila was dead, but right then I wanted it to be him so I could have the satisfaction of cuffing him and seeing him hauled off to the county lockup. I wanted the perverse joy of testifying at his trial and seeing him go away for a very long time.

I needed to go talk to Annie again, but my sitting here also served to emphasize that he wasn't to leave town. I had no legal basis to keep him here. I was trying to leverage my long position as police chief to get him to stay.

Yes, I was intimidating him. Yes, it wasn't the most noble use of my power or my office. But it seemed to me that he deserved it.

"Ortega to Carter," my radio squawked. "I found a witness for you. I think you should get up here. Over."

SIXTEEN

1:23 PM CHRISTMAS DAY. MARIN RESIDENCE

Deputy Ortega looked happy. She stood outside a small house, a cottage really, high on Carter Hill. She had a smile on her face that lit up her eyes.

I didn't like it. This was not a happy day, not a thing in this day to be happy about.

"What did you find?" I asked. "Why couldn't you tell me over the radio?"

"What if the murderer has a police scanner?" she asked, staring at her feet, her voice low. "Tiny town like this, you know, wouldn't be surprised."

She scuffed her foot on the cracked blacktop smushing around some snow, her arms crossed like she was cold. Was she shy? It was an odd temperament for law enforcement, but what she said showed intelligence.

"True enough," I said, and she looked up and that smile was back. "Now tell me what you know." The smile evaporated.

"Been knocking on doors," she began, licking her lips. "Nice little town you've got here, by the way. I was striking out, but I have to say no one freaked on seeing someone in a uniform at their door on Christmas morning."

She paused as if she wanted me to comment on that. I just stood there staring at her and she looked away, through the gap in the houses out toward the desert.

"Surprising lack of cameras, too. Like, two doorbell cameras but nothing we could use to see traffic on the street." She nodded at the cottage. "But the couple who lives here, the Marins, were out walking early this morning. They strolled over to Main, they wanted to see the Christmas lights. Kind of weird hour for a stroll if you ask me, but it fits them. Anyway, they heard a rather loud discussion up on the hill."

My heart was thumping and her voice sounded loud. This right here is often what cracks a case. Not a brilliant detective but the boring work of turning every stone.

And that's good for someone like me. I'm not brilliant. But I am stubborn and I do know my town.

"Figured you'd want to interview them yourself," she said with a shrug and a shy smile as she looked at me again.

I did my best to smile back, but I doubt it even qualified as a grimace. "Good work, Ortega."

She smiled widely and looked even younger, like some kid who just got their first bike or something.

I took a step towards the house. It was made of stone, local volcanic rocks giving it a dark, rough texture. The door was painted purple and Tibetan prayer flags were strung along the edge of the small patio roof.

"Can I join you, Boss?" she asked.

I stopped, my brain working. Lester and Annabelle were

doing what they could, but I couldn't send them out into the field. This deputy may be young, but she appeared to be competent.

"You know what," I said. "I've got another job for you."

Her eyes widened and she nodded. "What is it?"

"The way I see it, if we get close, the murderer is going to bolt. I want you waiting for them."

She nodded eagerly.

"Only one road here, and there's this curve about three tenths of a mile past the edge of town where you can park and not be seen," I said. "It's still 25 MPH there and everyone speeds. Let me give you a list of the vehicles to look out for."

She nodded again but just stood there.

"Don't you need to take notes?" I asked.

She shook her head. "Nah. Good memory."

So I ran down the suspect list, gave her the descriptions of all their cars and what they looked like.

"I won't let you down, Boss," she said. She took a step towards her vehicle. It was a newer Ford SUV with "SHER-IFF" painted on the side and a modern low-profile light bar on the top. It wasn't lost on me that it was much nicer than the old SUV we had.

She turned back when she got to the vehicle. "Got a name for this operation?" she asked.

"What?" She really caught me off guard with that question.

"So, you know," she said, a shy look on her round face. "When we talk on the radio other folks won't know what I'm doing."

What the hell? I just stared at her. I had no words.

"Sorry," she said, her strong shoulders slumping. "Just thought it'd be fun."

I don't know that I get the young. But part of my job is to try to understand the people that work for me so I can properly motivate them. "No," I said. "That is a good idea. You think about it while you're down there. You can tell me the first time we talk on the radio."

A smile lit up her face and she looked like a different person. She gave me an enthusiastic nod and got into her vehicle.

I watched her go. She was a curious young woman, but I had a feeling I could rely on her.

———

FELICIA AND HAROLD MARIN WERE OLD HIPPIES. I SAY THAT affectionately. They met during the "summer of love" in 1967 and, although their skin has wrinkled and their hair has grayed, they are still very much the same.

"Can I get you some tea?" Felicia asked. She was almost seventy now and her green eyes weren't quite as sparkling as they once were, but she was still tall and willowy.

"Yes, please," I said. I hated their tea, to tell you the truth. It would be some herbal concoction designed to help me relax that tastes like freshly mowed grass. But Felicia had a sweet quality to her and I had a hard time saying no to anything she offered.

"It's a tragedy, man," Harold said. "Lila was such a bright spirit. I gotta hope in my heart that her sweet energy is still with us." He was six inches shorter than Felicia with a powerful build that had gone soft. His long grey hair was tied back into a ponytail. He was barefoot and wearing a pink robe that showed off his hairy legs.

We were sitting in the cramped living room of their home. An old iron potbelly stove sat in a corner providing heat. I was on the red futon couch and Harold sat in an antique rocking chair nearby while Felicia was rattling around in the kitchen.

The only nod to the season was three poinsettia plants lined up on the dark wood coffee table.

"It is a tragedy," I said. "Lila was an important part of our town. She will be missed."

With the preponderance of rainbow colors and the whiff of marijuana in the air, you'd be inclined to file them under "Hippie: Clichéd." But they were both lawyers, and good ones at that, and could afford a much bigger house, but chose to live here and do a lot of charitable donations, not to mention the pro bono cases.

"This is a stain on our beautiful mountain," Harold said. "A blight that will bear horrible fruit if the culprit is not found and quickly."

"Which is why I am here," I said. "Sorry to bother you guys on Christmas."

He shrugged. "Jesus's birthday observed. A fine day to celebrate peace and love, but so is every day on our beautiful blue marble of a planet."

Harold and I chatted some more until Felicia returned with tea. She served the hot beverage in chunky pottery glazed a lovely shiny blue made by a Carterville local. It smelled like grass, but also like lemon, so I was hopeful that I could be at least a little graceful when I drank it.

Felicia sat next to me on the futon, her lips pursed. "This must be an awful burden for you, Henry."

I nodded.

"We know how special Lila was to you," she added.

And that just made my stomach churn, rebelling against the sandwich Annabelle had fed me. Did Annie's issue with my relationship with Lila have merit?

"Lila was special to us all," I managed to say.

I took a sip of tea to try to cover what must be written on my face and burned my tongue.

"Deputy Ortega told me you guys heard something last night," I said, pulling out my notebook, pen, and recorder. "Do you mind if I record our conversation?"

Harold cleared his throat. "I trust this is not a deposition?"

"No," I said. "The recording is for me."

"Will it be part of the official record of this case?" Felicia asked.

The hippies were gone and the lawyers were here.

"Let's just skip the recording," I said, putting the recorder back in my jacket pocket. "Can you tell me what happened last night?"

———

I LEFT THE MARINS AND WALKED OVER TO MAIN, THE WORDS OF Felicia and Harold rumbling around my head. I needed to be where they were to try to understand what they told me.

They lived on Engelmann Street. Only Fir is higher on Carter Hill, but still they were about 150 yards away from the site of the murder.

But it was early in the morning, a bit after 1:00 AM, and the murder site was about three hundred feet above them, and sound can travel in interesting ways.

"It was a fight," Harold had said. "No doubt about that."

"A man and a woman," Felicia added. "I'd like to say I'm sure the woman was Lila, but I can't. Last night I wouldn't have been able to tell you, but knowing what happened, now in my memory it sounds like her."

I stood on the corner and looked up Main Street. It goes up one short block to Fir and then jogs to the left for the switchback up to Carter Overlook. Where Main turned, the metal stairs that led to the overlook stood out in the sunlight.

The site of the murder wasn't visible, just the rock-walled edge of the overlook on top of the hill.

"We couldn't hear the words," Harold had said. "I mean, you know, not too many of them."

"But a few," Felicia added.

"'It's mine,'" Harold said. "The man shouted, 'it's mine, goddammit, it's mine.'"

"Do you know what that means?" Felica had asked.

I didn't tell them, but my heart broke when I heard them say it. They didn't know Lila was pregnant, but I did. They didn't know who the father was, but I did.

I pulled out my phone and texted Annabelle, "Update?"

The radio didn't seem to be private enough and I had instructed them to have all conversations on the speaker-phone. I had made it so I couldn't have a private conversation with Annabelle.

But Lester couldn't have done it, could he? But even if he hadn't, he left out his shouting match with Lila from what he told me. I mean, it was likely that they heard him up there. He left the party before I did and before Lila did. He could have been up there waiting for her to come out, his mind having spent too much time thinking about the baby she carried, about the family he never had.

I stared at my phone willing a text from Annabelle to pop up, my stomach clenching and my heart beating hard.

"Come on," I hissed, shaking my head.

There wasn't time. Why had I agreed to Annabelle's plan? Why had I spared precious moments walking over here?

I cursed and jogged back to the SUV.

I was getting out of the SUV, about to barge into Annabelle's house when my phone chimed. It was a text message from Annabelle.

"We found something. Can you get over here?"

I closed the car door and took a moment trying to get my heart to slow down. Trying to banish images of Annabelle laid out on her fancy oriental rug with a hole in her neck, blood staining the carpet and crawling slowly over the floor while a crazed Martin Lester stood over her.

I took a moment to think it through. If Officer Lester was the murderer then…

Then I was a terrible judge of character.

Then I let an unbalanced man work as a police officer in my town for years.

Then I had put Annabelle in horrible danger.

Then I had put Deputy Ortega at risk by posting her down on Carterville Road waiting for one of the suspects to speed by, including Martin Lester who would be armed and the best shot of anyone I've ever known.

Innocent or guilty, I needed to get Lester away from Annabelle and lock him up without anything else terrible happening today.

Lester wasn't dumb. He didn't talk all that much and his words came slowly, but that didn't make him dumb. If he was the murderer, he was in there trying to find a way out.

I got out of the SUV, slipped the taser off my belt, and shoved it into my back pocket. I stood there in the cold, letting the sun warm my face and counted slowly to ten. It wouldn't be good if I showed up at her door seconds after she texted.

My brain was on fire, spinning in circles. I wasn't thinking as clearly as I would have liked. I couldn't believe that my friend and colleague was capable of murder, but then again, I hadn't believed he would keep a secret like being the father of Lila's child from me. Especially after she turned up dead. But he did.

And Annie was on my mind too. She didn't have an alibi, she had left out important information during our interview. I wanted to go confront her with it, but the distractions kept mounting.

I thought back to Lester's odd behavior up on the hill this morning. I had thought it was just him seeing someone dead that he knew, his inexperience with this kind of crime. But it wasn't just that, was it?

It hadn't been long enough, but I couldn't wait. I walked to her door and knocked.

"Well that was certainly quick," Annabelle said with a smile as she opened the door. When she saw my face, the smile evaporated. "What is it, Henry?" She brushed her bright red hair behind her ear, a frown taking over her face and pulling down her red lips.

I could see Lester sitting in the living room near the stove, papers and a couple of laptops arranged on the coffee table, a coffee cup in his hand.

"Lester," I whispered, my eyes widening.

Annabelle suddenly looked ten years older as the color drained from her face. "No," she mouthed.

"Not sure," I whispered. "Could be."

"You all going to stop whispering and tell me what's going on?" Lester said from the couch. He sounded tired.

"I've got some new information on the case," I said, trying to sound as normal as possible.

"Good," he said with a grim smile. "So do we. It looks like Arnold Hughes was blackmailing Lila Chang."

My heart thumped in my chest, and I swear it stopped. The whole moment froze. Annabelle had turned to look at Lester. Lester was waving a phone in the air and looking at me. They must have figured out a way to unlock Lila's phone. His eyes widened like he could see what we were thinking.

His dull blue eyes flicked from me to Annabelle and back again, his mustache sagging down into a frown, his hand going to his belt and then stopping as he raised his hands slowly into the air.

My heart thumped again and time restarted with a painful lurch.

"I didn't do it," he said. "I swear to God, I didn't kill Lila. I ain't no killer."

EIGHTEEN

2:38 PM CHRISTMAS DAY. CARTERVILLE POLICE DEPARTMENT

LESTER WAS WHITE AS A GHOST, HIS SKIN PALER THAN HIS mustache as he gazed out from the holding cell in the Carterville Police Station.

He had come peacefully, letting me disarm him and cuff him. He had wanted to start talking right then, like when he had told me he was the father of Lila's child, but I read him his rights and told him to shut the hell up.

I still didn't know if he had done it, all I knew was that he lied to me. And I was furious about that. I arrested him because I needed him locked up and off the board. There were too many players, too many suspects, and I needed to focus.

My heart thumped in my head, a spiking pain in the back of my left eye. I longed for more coffee but that would make it worse.

No. Scratch that. What I longed for was an unreasonable

amount of gin and a sleep so deep nothing would wake me up.

"Are you sure you don't want a lawyer?" I asked him.

He shook his head. He was slumped on the narrow bed, his blue uniform looking very out of place behind steel bars.

"Can you please state your answer for the record," I said.

He looked up and glared at me briefly. "No. I don't want no damn lawyer."

The cell smelled like stale beer with a whiff of vomit. Clint Ryan had slept it off and was back home, but his scent lingered.

The immensity of this day hit me again. Hard. Making my chest hurt. "Shit, Martin," I said with a sigh. "Shit."

"I didn't kill her," he said.

I nodded. I wanted to believe him. "But I need you in that cell," I said. "You understand that, don't you?"

"Oh sure," he said with a resigned nod. "If I ain't the killer you're afraid I'll go after them once this gets sorted."

"Right," I said, feeling some small relief.

"But I ain't the killer and you are wasting your time," he said.

The little recorder was running and sitting on the floor. I was in a chair, an old, uncomfortable wooden chair. I could hear Annabelle tapping on a computer in the office behind us. I had unrecused her. If she was the murderer, I was screwed anyway, and I needed the help.

Annabelle had managed to unlock Lila's phone. She had tried a new unlock code every minute or two until she found one that worked. It was 742742. If you map numbers to letters her code was "PGCPGC." She loved her little shop.

Annabelle was leveraging the unlocked phone to recover

passwords and get into her social media accounts and her email. To look for more evidence of Arnold Hughes blackmailing her. To look for communications Martin Lester might have made with her.

We were pushing things here. Since Lila was deceased, the Fourth Amendment didn't really apply to her and a search warrant was in the works anyways, but it didn't feel like we had the time. This murder needed to be solved.

"You didn't tell me everything," I said, leaning back, the old wood of the chair creaking a bit. "You had a fight with Lila up on the hill." I flipped open my notepad. "At just after 1:00 AM. You were heard yelling, 'It's mine, goddammit, it's mine.'"

And, yes, I had made an assumption. The Marins had not IDed Lester, but it had to be him.

He looked even paler as he slowly nodded, his head raising and his eyes meeting mine. They were so pale, his blue eyes looked almost grey. I felt a shiver and it almost seemed like he was a ghost.

"I left the party at around eleven," he said. "You were still sitting there at one of the tables, wrung out by Annie Smith. Again. But I didn't leave. Lila said she wanted to talk. She had whispered it to me earlier. Said something had happened. Something bad."

I scribbled a few notes and nodded for him to continue.

"Lila was my friend," he said, anger starting to light up his features as he leaned forward. "I loved her. She got me. A lot of people in this town don't."

The look he gave me felt like an accusation. And I probably deserved it. Lester just turned fifty-nine, and while the world had changed a lot, it must have been hard to grow up in a small town and be different. When I went to high school, one boy would accuse another of being gay (with words far worse than that) as an insult. It must have been a lot worse for him.

And we never talked about his sexuality. Maybe he didn't feel safe talking to me about it. We were colleagues, first and foremost, but I always considered us friends. But, apparently, not the kind of friends that can talk about who they really are.

I blame the job. I was friendly with most everyone, but how many people were actually my friends?

I shoved all of that down. There would be time to reflect on all of this after we found Lila's killer. Preferably with a real friend and a drink or two.

"So walk me through what happened after you left me at the party," I said. My voice was even but my heart was thumping away.

He nodded and leaned back. "She said to wait for her. So I waited. Over by the church. You had left, almost everyone had left, by the time she came out."

"You waited from 11:00 PM to 1:00 AM outside in the cold?" I asked.

He sighed and nodded. "I'm too damn old to be a father, but I ought to have enough years left to help out. Teach the kid somethin'. So if Lila thought she was in trouble, I was going do everything in my power to help her. What's a couple of hours in the cold for her, for the baby?"

I wrote a few notes and nodded for him to continue. If he was by the church for that long, there would be tracks, evidence.

"When she came out of the tent, I walked over," he said. "But the cold, it had gotten to me. I had been pacing. Nervous. Imagining the worst. 'What is it?' I asked.

"She shook her head and whispered, 'Not here,' and drug me over towards the woods."

"Where was this in relationship to where her body was found?" I asked.

He shrugged. "Just down the road, not far from the parking lot on the south side of the road towards the edge of the hill."

I made a note. If they walked off the road, there would be more tracks to find. "What happened?"

He took a breath and his mustache wagged like he was chewing on his lip again. "She told me someone had found out that Lila Chang wasn't her real name, that they had threatened to tell her ex-husband where she was. She told me she was going to leave town and I would never see her again."

"And the baby," I added. "You would never see the baby."

He nodded, his eyes fierce again. I have a son, so that was a look I could relate to. If my wife had told me that when she was pregnant, I would have lost it. Completely. Even before she was showing, I was so in love with that baby, it was ridiculous.

Now take Martin Lester staring at sixty and having the opportunity he thought he never would have ripped away from him. Would that drive him to murder?

"I asked her who it was," he said, "but she wouldn't tell me. We know now it was that snake, Arnold Hughes, but she wouldn't tell me. I told her I would protect her, but she didn't believe me. I offered to go with her, to leave this life and change my name too, but she..." He trailed off and ended up staring at the stained cement floor of his cell.

I gave him a few breaths, but when he didn't continue, I said, "She what?"

"She laughed at me," he said quietly.

I didn't say a word, and Annabelle's typing suddenly stopped. She was listening in. I didn't dare breathe. Martin Lester had opportunity and now he had motive.

His mouth moved but he didn't say anything. And then he sighed and sniffed. "She laughed at me," he said again. "And I've been thinkin' about it a lot. Trying to remember exactly what it sounded like, trying to recall the exact look on her face."

He looked up at me and I couldn't even read his expression. His pale face looked haunted and resigned and furious all at the same time. "'Cause right then," he continued, "it sounded like the way people have always laughed at me and I got mad. I yelled. I said what the Marins heard, I said, 'It's mine too, goddammit, it's mine too.' There was more. She was scared. We fought."

He swallowed hard and continued. "But I don't think that is the way she meant it. I think she was surprised. I think maybe she was letting out some of the energy that had her all twisted up. I think that if I hadn't yelled at her that she would have let me help her, that she would still be alive."

He slumped back onto the bed and started quietly weeping. His tears tugged at me because I wanted to cry too. For his loss. For my loss. For Carterville's loss.

NINETEEN

3:26 PM CHRISTMAS DAY. CARTERVILLE POLICE DEPARTMENT

I clicked off the recorder and left Martin Lester be. He needed to grieve, but it wasn't time for me to grieve yet. I grabbed Annabelle and we went into my office, leaving the door opened just a crack so we could hear if someone came into the office.

I was sitting behind my messy desk, my little notebook in hand, and Annabelle sat across from me, her laptop out.

"Arnold Hughes," I said. "What do we know?"

"That damn snake, he needs to go to jail," Annabelle offered tartly, her southern accent adding bite.

I just raised my eyebrows and didn't say anything else. I was tired of words. I wanted action. I wanted to go arrest someone.

Annabelle nodded. "This is mostly from emails, a little from texts. In April, one of Lila's employees badly burned their hand on that espresso machine of hers."

I nodded. I don't remember the young lady's name, but I remember hearing about it. She was a college student from Northern Arizona University in Carterville working on the weekends.

"Hughes handled the insurance for Lila's business," Annabelle said, flicking away at her laptop screen. "Liability and worker's comp came into play here."

"Sounds about right," I said. "So what's the problem?"

"The problem is, according to Arnold Hughes, that her bills were four months behind when this happened," she said.

I leaned forward. "But…?"

"But Lila claims to have paid them," Annabelle said, a sneer twisting her red lips.

Insurance fraud. Now we had motive for Arnold Hughes.

"Let me guess," I offered. "Ole Arnie convinced Lila to pay her bills in cash, which she would have from the business, but somehow things didn't end up getting paid."

Annabelle nodded, the muscles on her jaw working.

"She must have been pissed," I said.

She kept nodding. "These emails and texts, they aren't the entirety of the conversation, but there are hints here. From what I can tell she threatened to tell you and he threatened to tell her ex-husband exactly where she was and what she was doin' and what her new name was."

Names are strange things. Sure it didn't surprise me that Lila had changed her name, that "Lila" wasn't that name she was born with, but it would always be her name to me. Anything else wouldn't sound right.

Last night Lila had said to me, *Some shit went down earlier in the year so I negotiated a lower price on my lease.* That shit was this problem with her insurance which must have drained her reserves and forced her to negotiate a lower lease with Karen Winslow, which resulted in the raising of her rent.

But Lila was running a business. You have to properly account for expenses, including cash outlays. "Are there any references to receipts for the cash?" I asked. "Arnie must have given her some."

Annabelle nodded eagerly. If we could find evidence of the fraud, that would make all the difference. She tapped away and flicked on the screen some more. Not sure how she could do either so well with those long red fingernails of hers, but she managed just fine. "I don't see nothin'," she said.

Damn. And even if Arnold Hughes was guilty of insurance fraud, it doesn't mean he was guilty of murder. I stood up. "That's not enough to do anything yet, but keep at it. And we'll need that search warrant expanded to Lila's business records."

Annabelle gave me a grim nod as I walked out of the office. "Where are you goin'?" she asked.

I turned and gave her a grim smile. "I've got a few more questions for Martin and then I'm off to have another fun-filled conversation with Annie Smith. She left something important out of her statement."

———

"HUGHES IS GOING TO GO DOWN," I SAID TO MARTIN LESTER, his head down as he slumped on the narrow bed of his cell. "I'm sure of it."

I was talking about insurance fraud and I was only fairly

sure, but I felt for the guy and I wanted to give him some good news.

He sniffed and looked up. His red-rimmed eyes made me want to look away, but I held his gaze. "He did it," Lester said.

I ignored his assertion and asked, "Tell me what happened when you left Lila."

He looked away. "We fought. It wasn't pretty. Things were said. I walked back to my truck, and when I drove by, she was still standing there."

"In the same place you fought?" I asked.

He nodded.

"Was she wearing a jacket?" I asked.

He looked surprised and nodded. "Yeah. The same green one she always wears with her elf outfit."

That had been bothering me. It was cold last night. Why was her body found without a jacket? I sat back down in the old wooden chair and scooted it closer to Lester, the sound of wood scraping on the cement loud.

"Why didn't you tell me right away this morning?" I asked. I had forgotten to turn the recorder back on. I let it be. I could ask these questions again later if I needed them for the record.

He shrugged and looked down at his shoes. "I figured I'd end up here. Useless. And I know I didn't do it." He looked back up to me. "Do you believe me?"

"I want to, Martin," I said. "But you know this job. Belief doesn't matter much here, evidence does."

He gave me a resigned nod and slumped back.

We chatted a bit. Just normal stuff, like what our families were doing today. At first it was stilted, and then the words flowed like they usually do, meaning a bit slowly, but we had a conversation that had nothing to do with murder.

You might be wondering why in the world I would take the time right then and right there to do that. Well, it's pretty simple. I needed a break, a moment that was not about Lila's death. And I needed to experience Martin Lester as my friend again. Because I knew Annie Smith was next.

TWENTY

3:40 PM CHRISTMAS DAY. CARTERVILLE INN

The lobby of the Carterville Inn used to be a saloon back in the late 1800s. The inn sits right on the Circle and is one of the older buildings in town.

The long counter, made of local pine, was the bar. The historic black and white photos on the walls invoke the feeling of old Carterville. Like many modern hotels, the space serves multiple purposes. And when I walked in, the scent of coffee, bacon, and sugar wafted over me.

The back of the room was set up with long tables, a few tourists still sitting there lingering over a late Christmas brunch. The tables were covered in festive red tablecloths and crowded with the remnants of their feast. Half-full champagne glasses, balled up napkins, a few plates, and remains of some recently opened Christmas presents.

I stood at the entrance for a moment watching Annie bustle back and forth clearing tables, pouring champagne, wearing a friendly smile. She was in her uniform of black and white. Black pants and a white dress shirt with a thin black tie and black vest.

The young blonde-haired Kennedy was dressed the same and attending to the guests that still lingered.

This was another scene in the Carterville Christmas snow globe, and I felt a sharp pang in my chest. I wanted to be part of the idyllic scene. I wanted to be sipping coffee and laughing, my belly full of good food.

I let the moment be and breathed in the lovely smells. I wanted this to be my morning. A man coming to see the woman he loves and watching her as she worked. Marveling at her grace, knowing that she ran a complicated business with seeming ease, longing to hold her and touch her and whisper things to her that made her laugh.

It was a silly indulgence. The world of today was very different than the world of yesterday. Not that I should be surprised. That's what the world does. It changes on you, dramatically, without regard to your needs or preferences.

Annie froze when she saw me, a brief look of guilt passing over her face before a frown took hold. She swept over and said, "What do you want, Henry?"

It took me a moment. I had been lost in what we used to be and wasn't ready for what we were. "I have some more questions for you," I said.

Her eyes darted back to her customers and then her dark eyebrows raised. "About…?"

I nodded. Her blue eyes met mine and softened briefly and I remembered what Arnie had said, "She's still stuck on you."

It wasn't a useful thought, bringing with it a load of regret.

Her eyes hardened again. "Can you give me a minute?"

I nodded and she was gone, a smile on her face as she checked on her guests and talked to Kennedy.

When she came back, her frown was firmly in place and she led me into her office, a cramped space smaller than mine through a door just behind the bar.

"What is it?" she asked, her arms crossed as she leaned against her messy desk with more paperwork stacked on it than was stacked on mine.

I pulled out the recorder and my little notepad and gave her a questioning look. She nodded.

I started the recorder and said, "December 25, 2017, 4:13 PM, continuation of the interview between Henry Carter and Annie Smith regarding the murder of Lila Chang."

I took a breath, wishing I wasn't here doing this right now. "I talked to Arnold Hughes," I began.

She shrugged and nodded for me to continue.

"He indicated that you…" I glanced at my notes. "That you used your powers to put him to sleep at 12:49 AM. Is that true?"

She blinked and then her forehead furrowed. Her mouth opened and then she clamped it shut, her cheeks flushing just a touch. "Wait?" she said. "He said I knocked him out?"

I nodded and then remembered the recorder. "Yes. He said he was having trouble sleeping because of indigestion. He described it very specifically."

"I did no such thing," she said. "He had indigestion. He asked me to help him sleep and I told with all that he had drunk he would probably piss the bed if I did. He told me not to bother, went to the bathroom, and was soon snoring."

Was this a lie on Hughes's part, or did he think that Annie actually did something? Or was Annie lying?

"Mr. Hughes also stated that he woke up alone, that you had left," I said, aware of how formal my words were. It felt awkward, but among the many things that were awkward between Annie and me, it was a small thing. "Is that true?" I asked.

She nodded, biting her lip. She knew what it meant.

"Can you please speak your answer?" I asked.

"Yes," she said with a sigh. "Arnie was asleep when I left."

"What time was that?" I asked.

"About 5:30," she said. "This is a busy day here, and since my plans had changed and I wasn't taking the day off..." She ended in a shrug.

That hurt. I was her changed plans. I forged on. "Did anyone see you leave Mr. Hughes's house?" I asked. I felt bad about asking. My gut told me that Annie didn't do it. My gut also told me that Annie wouldn't be stuck on me much longer if I kept asking questions. But this was my job.

She bit her lip and shook her head. And then remembering the recorder, she said, "No."

"I assume there are witnesses to your arrival here shortly after," I said.

She nodded and said, "Yes."

I clicked the recorder off and just stared at Annie. I couldn't read her face, it was a hard mask and we were down to single syllable answers. I wanted to hold her, to share this sad moment for our town with her. I wanted to ask how she was doing.

The moment stretched out as we just stared at each other. What she had done in her anger by jumping into bed with Arnold Hughes was quite egregious. I understood her well enough for it to make sense, for it to be something Annie

Smith would do. But she did it to me. And it hurt. And that had been her intention.

The images of them dancing last night floating above the floor came back, except they were naked and kissing. I turned away. It seemed like there might be an opportunity to be "on again" here, but how was I supposed to let that go? How was I supposed to feel like I was enough for her?

My radio squawked to life. "Ortega to Carter, Operation Jack Rabbit has snared its first victim. Over."

I looked back at Annie, her arms were crossed and a frown decorated her face, but I swear I saw something different in those blue eyes of hers.

"I've got to go," I said.

She didn't say anything, just pursed her lips and nodded.

TWENTY-ONE
3:58 PM CHRISTMAS DAY. CARTERVILLE ROAD

Here's the thing to keep in mind about murderers. Most of them are not very good at it. Think about it. Practice makes perfect, and who gets to practice murder? Sure, you can watch every murder mystery ever made and that'll teach you a few things that are worthwhile, but mostly fill your head with a load of crap.

And sure, you might think you know what it feels like to have done something like that and lie to the police about it, but you don't. You know intellectually, but you don't know what it's going to feel like. You don't know what that sweat running down your neck, your heart thumping hard, your throat feeling dry will make you do.

Which is why I stationed Ortega where I did. No one in Carterville is good at murder, and I was hoping they would make a mistake.

Another mistake, that is. I'm sure there was a mistake in the murder which I had yet to find.

And I guess I should amend that "no one is good at murder" statement. It's too black and white, which almost nothing in this world is. A sociopath or a psychopath (not always sure what the difference is) could be good at murder because the feelings won't matter to them. They could execute a plan in a cold and calculated way.

But I wasn't expecting a sociopath or a psychopath as I headed out of Carterville. I was expecting a man trying to escape an arrest because of insurance fraud and, maybe, murder.

I hadn't asked Ortega for any more details over the radio. Time was tight, I didn't want her doing anything crazy to hold them, and she had me thinking about the radio and how others might be listening. Besides, it was a three-minute drive.

But it wasn't Arnold Hughes that Ortega had pulled over but Karen Winslow in her shiny silver Ford F-250.

We were about a hundred yards past that sharp turn on a straightaway flanked with tall junipers. I could smell just a whiff of them despite the cold, and that reminded me of gin and that made me wish I was home in front of the woodstove with a stiff drink.

Ortega was still in her sheriff's vehicle when I pulled behind her. I strolled up. "How fast was she going?" I asked.

"Thirty-nine," Ortega said with a conspiratorial grin. She showed me the radar gun.

"Good work. Go ahead and write up the ticket," I said. "I'm going to go have a chat with her."

The young woman looked a bit surprised and then nodded. The least I was willing to let Karen Winslow leave here with was a speeding ticket.

"And nice code name," I said, somehow remembering to be a decent human being.

She beamed at me. The girl just sucked up the praise. I had to wonder if she wasn't being properly managed over at the county. "Issue the ticket as normal after I'm done."

"Happy to, Boss," she said, the smile still lighting up her face.

I walked up slowly to the big truck. I would be surprised if Karen didn't have a gun in there. I would also be surprised if she tried anything. But caution is always warranted.

I saw her scowling at me in the big side mirror and did my best to keep my expression neutral. She rolled down the window as I pulled up next to her.

"Good afternoon, ma'am," I said with a tip of my hat. "Can I see your license and registration?"

"What the hell is the meaning of this, Henry?" she asked. I guess she didn't take kindly to me using the standard greeting on her.

I was tempted to continue the ruse, to treat her like I would a tourist. And that would be pleasant, but I didn't have the patience for it. "I told you not to leave town," I said. "You left town. And you were speeding. Fourteen miles over the limit, that's a pricey ticket. And as you know the CPD has a lean budget and we've got to get revenue where we can."

Okay. I had to have a little fun, didn't I?

She pursed her lips, her hazel eyes drilling into mine as she studied my face, trying to figure out how serious I was. She sighed and shook her head. "Ken called," she said. "There's an issue with Katie. She's hobbling around, probably the arthritis, but you know Ken is not great with the horses."

"But I told you not to leave town," I said.

She sighed. "It's five miles away. It's not even really leaving town."

I pointed back down the road. "The city limits are that way. You quite literally left town."

"And what are you going to do about it?" she asked.

"I'm going to let Deputy Ortega issue you a speeding ticket," I said. Her mouth opened up, but I kept talking. "And then you are going to turn around and come back to the department and you are going to answer more questions for me."

"But… I… You…" she stammered. You could almost see the steam coming out of her ears and you could certainly see her cheeks flushing. And truth was, I didn't have any questions for her, but I had a few minutes to think them up.

This was a murder investigation. She was a suspect without an alibi. And, yes, this was a bit of a pissing match between a mayor and a chief of police, but that's not all it was.

As I turned to go, I said, "And you best get out your license and registration for Deputy Ortega."

———

BACK IN MY VEHICLE, I WATCHED ORTEGA ISSUE THE TICKET. It's an everyday thing for a cop. And there is always some question as to what you will find when you approach a car you've pulled over. It's not like the movies and TV. It's almost always nothing more than a nervous driver who is hoping they don't get a ticket. Almost always.

Ortega approached the big silver F-250 with caution, even though there was little need for it. She was slow and wary, taking everything in. Looking down the two-lane blacktop, her eyes scanning the truck and the juniper forest behind it. As I watched her move, the "fireplug" impression increased. She was short and a bit round but clearly strong. Her walk wasn't cocky, but it was self-assured and confident.

This didn't quite jive with her shyness, and that apparent contradiction was fascinating.

I was sitting there, in part, to make sure Karen Winslow turned around and went back to town. I was observing Deputy Ortega because she was working for me and I needed a better feel for her. But mostly I was sitting there because I needed a moment. This day had been nonstop, and while I had plenty of suspects, two without alibis, and I knew a lot more of what had been going on, I really didn't know what had happened to Lila in the forest.

The engine was off and the near silence was soothing. It was cold, but the sun shining in through the windows felt good.

As I watched, my mind skipped around.

Lila Chang helping me find a present for Annie, but her eyes kept roaming and her smile wasn't as bright as usual. Maybe it was, in part, that Arnold Hughes had been her customer right before me. Maybe there had been a tense whispered conversation regarding her turning him in and him telling her ex-husband where she was.

Then the Silver Ball where Lila told me about her problems with Karen Winslow and the Carterville Brewery. But something else was bothering her then, too. Her eyes flicking around restlessly as if expecting to see someone she feared.

Now I know it was not only her conflict with Arnold Hughes but her pending conversation with Martin Lester where she would tell him that she was leaving town and he would never see her again. That he would never meet his baby.

And I missed it. I wasn't there for her when she needed me. There were plenty of hints, but I was too lost in the drama with Annie to see her and her needs clearly.

And then I remembered her body there slumped against the tree, her blood soaking into the crusty white snow, a "V" scratched in the snow as she died. Her elf costume and lack of a jacket.

What had happened after Martin Lester had driven off? How did she get back to where she died? Where was her jacket?

I know enough about the human ego to be clear that it is the part of us that makes everything about us. Makes us feel like the world revolves around us. But in this case, it really did feel like this was about me.

Don't get me wrong, Lila was the true center of this and I knew it, but my own personal and professional failures seemed to be coalescing in this mess. There would never be a time when someone on my watch was murdered and I wouldn't want to find the killer. But right here, right now, it felt like finding Lila's killer was the only way for me to move forward. From my personal and professional failures. The only way I could heal from this disastrous few days would be to find the murderer. And the only way our little town would be able to heal.

But there is no making things right after a murder. The life cannot be restored. But you can move forward, and I was desperate for it. To put this murder behind me. To put Annie behind me. To go back to the quirky policing a little town with a lot of people with powers requires.

It didn't take long for Ortega to issue the ticket, but it felt like it stretched out. Like I had been sitting here for an hour and I felt my body relaxing just a touch. The knots in my shoulders weren't as tight and I wasn't as desperate for a drink.

And then my phone bleeped, a text had come in, and my radio came to life. "Carter, this is Unger. I just sent you an urgent text. Please respond. Over."

The urgency in Annabelle's voice made her southern accent more pronounced.

I picked up my phone and unlocked it with my index finger. The text read, "Martin is gone," followed by a screaming face emoji.

I blinked, my quiet moment shattered and my mind skipping like an engine that wouldn't quite start.

Martin Lester was locked in a cell—how the hell could he be gone?

That didn't matter. What mattered was where he would go. And there was only one place.

PART 3

A KIND OF JUSTICE: CHRISTMAS DAY

TWENTY-TWO

4:18 PM CHRISTMAS DAY. HUGHES RESIDENCE

As a kid, I imagined tearing down streets with a siren blazing would have been a thrill.

I wasn't wrong. It is. But it's also tense and frightening and fraught with peril. There's a balance to be struck that is difficult when adrenaline is pouring through your veins.

After Annabelle's text, after my brain engaged, it was obvious where Martin Lester was going. To confront Arnold Hughes, and probably more.

As Ortega ambled back towards her vehicle, I started the SUV, backed up, my wheels kicking up the cinders that made up the thin shoulder, checked the road, and swung back around towards Carterville.

"This is Carter," I said into the radio as I leaned on the gas, the old SUV leaping forward. "Message received. Heading towards Hughes residence. Over."

I flicked on the sirens and gripped the steering wheel with

both hands. This Christmas already had one murder—I didn't want it having two.

And while Arnold Hughes was my preferred suspect, while he was the one my "gut" told me did it, my gut could not be trusted because of what happened with Annie.

"Be careful, Henry," Annabelle said over the radio, the worry in her voice apparent. The lack of "over" making it very clear she was rattled.

That idyllic snow globe that is Carterville, Arizona, looked a lot different then. I was scanning the road, looking for pedestrians and other vehicles.

I surged past the parking lot at the bottom of the hill on my left. Saw a flash of silver Airstreams nestled under junipers to my right were Mary and William Reilly were enjoying their Christmas. I slowed as I hit Carter Hill proper, the historic houses quickly being replaced by mostly historic buildings. The Carterville Diner on the left with its bright neon fifties-style sign looking out of place and welcoming too.

After the diner, the red brick buildings went from two stories to three. Another half block and I hit the Circle and slowed down. A blue Prius plodding along and forcing me to put my brakes on. They seemed unaware of my presence despite the sirens. I leaned on my horn and got as close as I dared.

In the Circle, I passed the Carterville Inn and on the other side of the Circle I saw Peaks Gifts and Coffee next to the Carterville Antique Shoppe. The lovely old building that Karen Winslow wanted to turn into a brewery. And attract more tourists who would come hoping to see someone use their powers.

Like Arnold Hughes and his levitation during the Silver Ball.

The damn Prius seemed to be totally clueless and the trip around the Circle seemed to take forever, giving me too much time to think, giving my adrenaline no outlet. After we exited the Circle, I zigged over to the left lane, stepped on the gas and zagged back in front of the Prius. The hill got steep again and I could hear it in the whine of the engine. It was working hard just like my heart as it clanged in my chest.

Up another block where the businesses turned back into houses and the hill steepened further.

I worried that I was going to be too late. That the Prius had cost me precious seconds. That I would find Arnold Hughes dead and Martin Lester standing over him, a ruined man.

Maybe Lester was already ruined, having lost Lila and his child. But committing cold-blooded murder would ruin him for sure. He was a quiet, introspective man. And while he didn't speak every thought that popped into his head, he felt deeply.

And Arnold Hughes wouldn't see it coming.

I told you I wouldn't speak of someone's power until it was relevant to the story. Well, I guess Lester's power is relevant now. I'm guessing it helped him escape the station without Annabelle knowing, and it would certainly help him sneak up on Hughes.

Lester was a quiet man and his power was one of those that seemed to fit, that seemed to amplify something already in the person. His power was the power of quiet.

Yeah. I know, that doesn't make a bit of sense. Let me try to explain.

Martin Lester can kind of disappear. Not really, but that's how it can seem. If he wants too, if he withdraws deeply into himself, he is very hard to see. He's not invisible or anything, he's not even silent. It's just that people won't notice him.

There are plenty of parties where most people will swear that Lester wasn't there and yet when you look at photos, there he was. He's not a party kind of a guy, his tendency is to withdraw into crowds.

And that's how we figured out his power. It was a Carter-ville Fourth of July celebration where he was in many pictures, but no one remembered seeing him.

And this power was actually very useful in his job. Most people, when they see a cop, get all tense and change their behavior. Lester can go anywhere and observe freely.

And that's why Arnold Hughes would never see him coming.

And if he found a way to get the cell door open—which he must have—that's how he got out of the CPD without Annabelle noticing.

Close to the top of Carter Hill, I turned left and headed down Engelmann Street, the same street I lived on but on the east side of the hill instead of the west. When I pulled into Arnie's driveway, it was chaos.

Hughes's car door was open, a rollable luggage case on its side near the open trunk. There was a garbage bag hanging halfway out of the trunk of the new Acura sedan, the black plastic torn and showing a cheery green inside.

Hughes's house was two stories, like most of the houses here, because of the narrow lots, with aged red bricks and a few Victorian touches that didn't quite fit to my taste. Christmas lights were strung all over the house. They were on and gave a strange counterpoint to what else was in the driveway. Martin Lester holding Arnold Hughes and pressing a knife to his throat.

Lester was showing too many teeth and Hughes was pale and looking much older than the last time I saw him. The knife, a folding pocketknife with a matte black handle, gleamed in the sunshine.

My heart thumped and my brain slipped. All I could think was, "Damn Prius." Maybe if I had gotten here a few seconds earlier this wouldn't be such a difficult situation.

Hughes wasn't struggling anymore, both of them still and staring at me. The dynamic had changed and they were both trying to figure out what it meant to have me here. My presence could push Lester further and Hughes was probably hoping I would save him.

I didn't want to. Seeing the conviction written on Lester's face, I wanted to leave Hughes, let this play out. And for a moment it was "Damn, Prius, you should have slowed me down more."

But that was a moment and not me. Not the job.

Even though my heart was bouncing around my chest like a pinball, I got out of the SUV slowly and said, "Merry Christmas, boys. What appears to be the problem here?"

In a cop's tool bag are a lot of violent options. I had a gun and a taser on me. These are not the first choice. Especially in a town like Carterville and with one of my own people. Escalation can happen quickly, and Lester knows me and knows the playbook.

It's not like some crazy movie where I would do a fast draw, shoot Lester in the leg and save justice for all.

First off, I'm not that good of a shot. Secondly, a shot to

the leg can kill you pretty quick. And thirdly, I didn't want any more bloodshed today.

Hughes started to speak, a stuttering, "I... He..." but Lester pressed the knife to Hughes's neck, and he squeaked in a way that would have pleased me under different circumstances.

"Report, Officer Lester," I said, my tone serious but not a shout or anything. He was the one I needed to talk.

"He did it," Lester said, nodding towards the back of the car. "I found Lila's jacket in his trunk. I walked up. I watched him. He was pacing out here. Chewing his fingernails like some scared little kid."

Lester was staring at me, his pale blue eyes looking more than a little haunted. "I was just going to watch, Henry," he said. "I swear to you. Just see if I could find some proof. But he kept checking his phone. Kept pacing. And then it was clear he was going to bolt. I... I had to stop him."

"That's some good work, Officer," I said. "Mind telling me how you got out of the cell?"

Sure, there were more pressing issues, but keeping Lester talking was what needed to happen right now.

"I let Clint Ryan out this morning after he sobered up," he said. "Still had the key in my pocket. It's not like you searched me, Chief."

I nodded and took a step forward. I felt a flush of shame for skipping something so basic, and decided to lean into it. "Damn," I said. "That was stupid of me."

I was being careful with my hands, keeping them in front of me and nowhere near my weapons.

"It was," Lester said.

"Like I was a rookie," I said, taking another small step

forward. I was about four feet away from the trunk. "You say that's Lila's jacket?" I asked.

"I'm sure of it," he said, which led me to believe he hadn't actually looked at it.

"Do you mind?" I asked, nodding towards the bag dangling out of the trunk.

It was a weird moment. Lester holding a knife to Hughes's throat and me acting like it was the most normal of things. It wasn't. The adrenaline flowing through all of our bodies was proof of that, but the smallest thing could push Lester over the edge.

I was inclined to believe his story, but I was aware that was partially me wanting to see Hughes suffer. And of the two of them, Hughes was the one with an alibi.

"Go ahead," Lester said.

Hughes started to speak, "He—" but Lester pressed the knife to his throat and he stopped. I pulled some latex gloves out of my pocket and slowly put them on.

"There's two of us here now," I said, nodding towards Hughes. "Maybe it'd be okay if you let him talk."

"He'll just try to lie his way out of it," Lester said, his voice shaking with rage.

"Yeah," I said putting the first glove on. "I suspect he will, but you know I'm going to have to hear what he has to say." I grabbed the recorder out of my jacket pocket with my ungloved hand and switched it on. "Look, we'll get it on tape."

Lester looked at me warily, but I just kept acting like this was an interview not a hostage situation. I cleared my throat and said, "December 25, 2017, 4:56 PM interview between Henry Carter, Martin Lester, and Arnold Hughes regarding the murder of Lila Chang this morning between 1:00 and 2:00 AM. Please state your names for the record."

They both stared at me. For a moment I thought I had gone too far, that the incongruity of this would push Lester over the edge, but then his face relaxed minutely and he said, "My name is Martin Lester."

I nodded at Hughes, his eyes wide. "Now let him speak, Officer Lester."

Lester backed off the knife slightly and Hughes said, "Mmmm my name is Arnie Hughes. I didn't do anything. I swear. That jacket… he—"

Hughes ended in a squeak as Lester pressed the knife to his neck again.

"Let him speak, Officer," I said. I put the recorder on the pavement and put the other latex glove on. When Lester didn't do anything, I added, "That's an order."

Lester wasn't right. He wasn't completely sane. And I had no idea what to do. So I had to trust my gut this time. This wasn't something I could intellectualize myself out of. I had known Martin Lester all my life. The quiet, gentle man. My near-daily companion as an officer and then as the police chief of Carterville. The expert marksman and dedicated historian of Northern Arizona.

He was doing a bad thing here and now, but he was a good man.

And seeing him like this, seeing him broken, I had to wonder if he could have killed Lila. I was still not trusting my gut on who the murderer was.

That "V" Lila drew could have been the start of an "M" for Martin or an "A" for Arnold.

Still he pressed the knife to Hughes's neck. "Please, Martin," I said, letting the fatigue of the day into my voice. "Please. This has been a hell of a twenty-four hours. Let the man speak. I promise you that I will bring the murderer to justice."

He blinked and nodded, pulling the knife away from Hughes's throat, a drop of blood clinging to the skin of his neck.

Hughes just stared at me. "You want to tell me about this jacket?" I asked as I slowly opened up the torn garbage bag.

It was Lila's jacket. The deep shade of green and the long cut of it made it clear. My stomach clenched and I wanted to hurt Arnold Hughes.

"He planted it," Hughes said. "I… I don't know where that jacket came from… I don't know where—"

Lester pressed the knife to Hughes's neck again.

I just glared at Lester and he eased the knife back. "Please continue," I said.

Hughes was terrified. He didn't trust either of us, and he was convinced he was about to die. I could see it in his flicking eyes as he looked at me and then at the recorder on the ground, and then roaming the street as if he was hoping for someone to come by and save him.

He wasn't used to being powerless. He wasn't used to being the victim. He had had money all his life. And good looks. And was used to talking himself out of any trouble his carelessness might land him in.

"He planted the jacket," Hughes said, the words rushing out of him as if he was afraid he wouldn't get the chance to finish them.

"That so?" I asked. "Did you see him plant it?"

After an aborted attempt to shake his head, he said, "No. But it wasn't there before. Everyone knows how sneaky Martin can be."

I pushed the bag all the way in the trunk and looked around. It was neat, like someone had vacuumed it out not too long ago. There was a first aid kit, a gallon of water, a blanket, and a cardboard box with some canned goods. The water wasn't frozen, he had loaded it recently.

I slowly took off the gloves. "Let's talk about last night," I said, pulling out my notebook and flipping it back a few pages. "You said you went to sleep at 12:49 AM and when you woke up Annie Smith was gone. What time was it that you woke up?"

Lester's brow furrowed like he was trying to figure out where I was going with this.

"I don't know," he said. "About 6:30. I got up and went to the bathroom and slept for another hour or so."

I nodded. "Annie Smith is a pretty sound sleeper," I said. "One of the benefits of her power. In my experience, sound enough for you to sneak out, drive up Carter Hill, and meet with Lila Chang."

"No," he said. "Why would I do that?"

Lester gave me the smallest of nods, encouraging me on.

"Oh, I don't know," I said. "Insurance fraud. You were blackmailing Lila with the threat of telling her ex where she was and what her new name was. You met in your car. The heater was running and Lila took her jacket off."

Hughes was staring at me, his eyes wide, his jaw working but no words coming out.

"I'm guessing she was pretty upset at the end of the conversation and left the car without her jacket," I said.

Hughes snorted, sounding like his usual confident self. "This is quite the fantasy you've got going on, Henry."

"Yeah. Probably," I said, taking a step closer. "Mind if I continue?"

"No. Please do," he said with a toothy smile. It seemed he had forgotten about the knife to his throat for a moment.

"You watched her leave," I said. "Maybe she told you she was going to come to me in the morning and tell me about her insurance problems. How you ripped her off. Maybe something in you just broke. You got out of the car and went after her."

I paused because I didn't understand the mechanics of the murder. How did Lila end up there with a hole in her throat, no murder weapon, and no tracks but her own?

"You stalked her," I said. "And you killed her."

He rolled his eyes. "And what about baby-daddy here?"

That one brought me up short. How did he know? He must have read the surprise on my face because he said, "She asked me to be the father before old Martin here. He's like a third string choice or something."

"You..." Martin said, his eyes wide and distant, the hand holding the knife drifting away. "She..."

I didn't know if it was true, but the pain on Lester's face was.

"Lila was a gullible little thing," Hughes said. "So trusting. A listening ear, a kind smile, and she opened right up. It was all business at first, but she soon confided in me. One night at the bar we were both there late, she was drunk. She told me about her ex. I smiled and listened, hoping for some fun later, but that didn't pan out.

"But I kept her secret and she trusted me. She asked me first."

"And you said no?" Lester asked. "How could you say no to her?"

Hughes snorted. "I'm not supporting some kid. And besides, she didn't want to get pregnant the old-fashioned way."

I took another small step forward. "So she trusted you enough to fall for your insurance scam?" I asked. "You talked her into paying you in cash. You gave her fake receipts. Didn't pay the insurance company."

He slowly shook his head. "Can you believe it? That she fell for that? It's just bad luck that that klutz employee of hers burned herself, otherwise no one would have known."

I was going to take another step closer, but something wasn't right. Hughes had pretty much confessed to insurance fraud with the recorder going. And I could see the emotions battling on Lester's face. Shock. Grief. Disdain. Anger. How long before he used that knife?

"She talked to me about it before she asked old man Martin here," he said, his eyes steady as he stared at me, a quirky smile playing on his face. "I told her that Martin would be loyal. Would probably leave everything to the baby. That he had good life insurance. That she should go for it."

I didn't know if this was true, but from the stricken look on Martin's face he thought it was. His arm relaxed further, his eyes wandering off. He was doubting everything he knew about Lila. Everything he thought his future was going to be.

It was bad enough that Lila and the baby were dead, now he couldn't even have the fantasy of what might have been.

I realized what Hughes was up to a moment before he acted. He was trying to hurt Lester, confuse him enough so that he would have a chance of survival. Hughes elbowed Lester in the stomach, the tall man doubling over. He ran in front of the car and around the house.

I gave chase.

TWENTY-THREE
4:25 PM CHRISTMAS DAY. HUGHES RESIDENCE

I'm quite sure I mentioned that Arnold Hughes was younger and fitter than me. He was running for his life. But I was running for justice.

It's a funny word, "justice."

I think most of us think that it means everything will be made right, the scales will be balanced, or some such thing as that. Like that image of the blindfolded woman holding up scales. Like this justice thing is absolute and always fair.

I know better.

If you go looking at the definition of the word, you'll see references to righteousness, equity, fairness, so you can be forgiven in thinking that justice served is a thing made right.

Lila's life was taken and that cannot be made right. There is no balancing that scale. The stand-in for justice is hunting down the murderer and locking them away. But one person's freedom does not balance the scales against another's life.

But justice is, like all things we humans strive for, an ideal.

A concept to reach for, even though we often fail. As flawed as our execution of the lofty concept is, we would be so much worse without it.

It's the striving for it that makes us better.

And even though the scales could not be balanced for Lila, I could try.

So as the younger, more athletic Arnold Hughes ran for his life, I ran for justice.

And Martin Lester may have thought he was running for justice, but he was running for revenge. The elbow to his gut slowed him down, but he moved too.

He was closer and we both came around the sedan at the same time. I leaned down and hit him hard in the side with my shoulder. The air whooshed out of him and he bounced off the side of the house and went down.

When you're the one seeking it, revenge can feel like justice, but it never is. Justice isn't personal—remember that image of the blindfolded woman with the scales?

I felt bad about doing that to Lester, but he had made it abundantly clear that I couldn't trust him in this matter.

But could I trust myself? This wasn't as personal to me as it was to Lester, but it was most certainly personal. These thoughts flickered through my head as I headed around the side of the house, through an open gate and onto Hughes's steeply sloping backyard. There was a deck to my left and the ground was covered in crunchy snow and slick, but what I saw almost pulled me up short.

Hughes was about ten feet in front of me as he leapt and started floating up into the air, his momentum carrying him away, like some helium filled balloon floating on the breeze.

If I hadn't been dealing with Carterville powers as long as

there have been Carterville powers, I would have stopped and just stood there and stared.

It was a sight. One moment he was running hard and the next he was floating off the ground, his momentum continuing to carry him forth.

It was a thing of wonder and beauty.

But I was running for justice so I ran harder, I used the downward slope of the yard to propel me faster. I jumped just as he was about to be out of my reach and I grabbed onto his right leg, my hands grabbing his ankle, and I was dangling there struggling to hold on. I wasn't floating like those ladies he danced with. And what the hell had I been thinking? That my weight would somehow counteract his power like he was a wayward balloon?

As I struggled to hang on, I reached higher, my hand making contact with the skin above his ankle, and…

And I was floating too.

Not being one of the "lucky ladies" that danced with him at the Silver Ball, I had never experienced his power. It was… How do I explain it? I was light, almost weightless, and it was amazing. I felt this giddy sense of happiness and just wanted to let out a laughter of pure joy.

I felt like anything was possible and like it was all going to be okay. I was floating. Over my beloved town. His yard passing below us and then the shingled roof of the next house appearing.

"No!" Hughes shouted, popping the bubble of my euphoria. I looked up and his free leg rose up and it was clear he was about to kick me. In the face. That'll sober you up, and quick.

We were about ten feet off the ground. We weren't going

up, but the hill was going down below us. In a few seconds we'd be just a couple of feet above his neighbor's roof, but I'd slide right off that steep roof and it wouldn't be pretty.

"Don't do it, Arnold!" I shouted.

He paused. "Why? My life is over, why shouldn't yours be too?"

Maybe he was professing a view of justice. A twisted one. A desire to take someone down with him. But maybe that would balance the scales for him. Seeing me maimed or killed would somehow make his eventual capture more palatable.

But that wasn't justice. The blind lady and the scales portray justice as a natural force that we humans strive for, not as something relative.

He was a man with nothing to lose. I ignored his question and just tried to keep him talking.

"Why?" I asked. "Why did you kill her?"

He looked down at me and blinked as if the question had caused some kind of malfunction in his brain. And then he looked confused and like he was about to start crying, like some little kid who had just fallen and skinned his knee. It made him look much younger than he was.

"You don't understand, Henry," he said slowly. "I would have lost everything."

I didn't bother telling him he was losing everything. I kept a hold of him, but realized my grip didn't have to be tight to keep floating with him. I just had to be touching his skin. I started to slowly release the grip of one of my hands.

"So explain it to me," I said.

The hill slid away underneath us, the closest roof ten feet below and then twenty.

I slowly let one hand go and… nothing changed. This gave

me options. I could reach my gun or my taser, but what good what that do? I looked up at Hughes and my cowboy hat slipped off my head. I reached for it with my free hand, but missed and watched it tumble to the ground, making it clear just what a long fall it had become.

My first thought, rather oddly, was that I was going to get a sunburn without my hat, my receding hairline making that an even greater possibility. And then I worried about people seeing me without my hat on and that aforementioned receding hairline. As the ground continued to slide away below us, I returned my hand and found my grip tightening even though it wasn't necessary.

"It was for only a few months that I didn't pay her insurance," he began. "I had invested in a venture and it was taking too long and I was short of cash. I mean, what harm would it do? Businesses like hers almost never use their insurance."

"What venture?" I asked. I know, it didn't seem like the most important thing, but something tickled in my mind.

"Karen's stupid brewery," he spat. "She promised lots of profits, but just kept needing more funds."

It's quite likely that Karen Winslow broke no laws, but it seemed to me that the scales needed to be balanced where she was concerned.

"That barista getting burned at PGC was some bad luck," I said. The nearest roof was over twenty feet below now. There was no surviving the fall.

He nodded.

"But why Lila?" I asked, letting the pain come out in my voice. "Why did you kill Lila? She never hurt anyone."

His brow furrowed and he looked like that kid who had

just skinned his knee again. "She wouldn't listen to reason. She was so upset. We fought. She stormed out. And I got so angry… It was like the anger took me over, owned me. There was a screwdriver in my glove compartment, I grabbed it and went after her. I…" He trailed off staring to the south out at the vast desert.

I no longer wondered how he did it. I could see it.

Lila had her second fight of the night in Hughes's car and stormed off. He grabbed the screwdriver and went after her. She had walked out into the forest and turned when she heard him coming.

He used his levitation power and floated over the snow, stabbed her with the screwdriver. He hit the tree we found Lila under, probably kicked off of it and floated back to the road. That's why there were no footprints besides Lila's.

We would have to find the screwdriver, which might have been in the trash bag with Lila's coat, but we had him on murder. Nothing would make Lila's death right, but it was something.

And then I barked out a laugh. We were 350 feet off the ground and almost to the Carterville Circle. It didn't seem possible that I was going to survive this. I could see people below pointing up at us. Probably tourists, thrilled to see a power in play.

This was making their Carterville Christmas. They probably thought it was a show for them, another flourish in the snow globe experience of Carterville.

And then it hit me. Arnold Hughes wasn't trying to get away… not really. He was trying to end it all, and he didn't need to kick me off because once we left the zone of influence, crossed the boundary where Carterville powers no longer worked, we would both fall out of the sky, making this a whole lot less like an idyllic snow globe.

TWENTY-FOUR

5:08 PM CHRISTMAS DAY. HIGH ABOVE CARTERVILLE

Arnold Hughes didn't want to die alone.

I can't say I blamed him. I didn't want to die alone either. I would have preferred my son or my sister by my side. Or, until this morning, Annie Smith.

At first, I refused to believe that the handsome, athletic, well-off, and self-assured Arnold Hughes would end it this way. But as we floated past Carterville and the ground was more than a thousand feet below us, I had to stop denying it.

Denial. One of the five stages of grief.

In this case, believing that Arnold wouldn't do it when he clearly would. When he was obviously going to. That was my denial.

I'm as human as the next person and have spent much of my life in denial. When the meteor hit, when the powers started, the whole town was in denial that something had happened. We wanted the old world to come back, but it was long gone.

Life does that to you. Changing dramatically and suddenly and it takes you a while to catch up. For some changes, I think that denial is protective, your psyche trying to give you time to catch up with the facts of your new situation.

But clearly Hughes wasn't in denial about his fate. One act of passionate violence and his world was over.

"Put us down, Arnold," I said, edging into the anger stage of grief. This wasn't the kind of grief you could take your time with. "Put us down, now!"

He just snorted and kept staring out over the desert. Due west of us was the northmost flank of the San Francisco Peaks, the sun sliding behind the tree-covered slopes, the blues of the sky deepening, and yellow and orange flaring up the edge of the mountain. No clouds to multiply the colors, but it was spectacular nonetheless.

My hand was slick with sweat but such was the nature of his power that I was in no danger of slipping.

"I'll shoot you in the leg," I said. "Clearly you want a quick and painless death. I can make sure that doesn't happen."

He shrugged but didn't look down at me. "Go ahead, Henry. Shoot me. I don't think I'll be able to hold my power and we'll end up the same way."

"Please, Arnie," I said, using his preferred name and slipping straight into bargaining. "You don't have to die today."

He looked down at me now and the angle I was viewing him from and the sneer on his face made him look positively evil. "First-degree murder is—what—twenty-five years to life? I'm not doing that, Henry. And don't ask me to put you down. I know the moment I do you'll taser me and haul me in."

He was right. I wouldn't use the taser unless I needed to, but if he put me down, I would take him in, so I didn't bother lying about it and slipped right into the depression stage. I was going to die. Today. On Christmas. There was no stopping it.

And I guess with this particular grief, depression was mixed liberally with acceptance. Not sure how I could have looked at my rapidly approaching death realistically and been anything but depressed.

It was silent as we floated along, the air cold, leaving me wishing I could zip my jacket up.

When Hughes leapt into the air from his yard, he had been running. Maybe four miles per hour. Given that the zone of influence, that area where Carterville powers worked, extended about five miles from town, we had a ways to go before we hit the boundary. Because it was clear that Hughes didn't have the guts to do it himself. Not directly. He was going to wait until his powers failed and we fell from the sky.

The breeze shifted and I could feel it on my face as I looked to the south and I silently started bargaining with the wind. Begging it to whip up and blow us back to the mountain. But that was unlikely. The wind usually blew down the mountain, not up it, and was more likely to speed our journey.

My radio squawked to life and I sucked in a breath in surprise. I had forgotten I had it on me. "Carter, this is Lester. Listen, Henry, you don't need to answer. I know you got your hands full right now, but I just wanted to say how sorry I am.

"This mess is my fault. If anyone should be up there, it should be me. I…"

He trailed off and I could hear the pain in his voice. It was an unusual display of emotions for the older man. Hughes was staring down at me, a worried look on his face, as if things could somehow get worse.

"I'm sorry," he continued. "I should have trusted you, Henry. I should have been honest about… her. I should have told you everything this morning. You ain't been nothing but kind to me your whole life."

His words were appreciated, but it was making the grief I was feeling over my impending end that much worse. He was reminding me of all I was about to lose.

"But, listen, I didn't radio you to be all maudlin and such. I wanted to let you know that we found the murder weapon. A bloody Phillips head screwdriver bundled up in Lila's jacket. And there's some blood-stained clothes in there too. We got Hughes dead to rights."

Hughes was staring at me, that kid with a skinned knee look on his face again. He wanted Lester to stop telling the truth. He wanted to escape. He was ready for it to end.

It was a fine line, this plan of his. It was clear that if he got pushed too far, he would do it himself and not wait for the edge of the zone of influence. So that had me wanting Lester to shut up too so that I got a few more minutes to live.

"There's more," Lester continued. "But I don't want to take up all your remaining time with it. I just wanted to thank you, Henry, for being so good to me and so good to the whole town for so many years. You… I…"

I could hear Lester sniff and take a deep breath.

"You will be missed. But the main thing I wanted you to know is the case is solved, so, in some strange way, things are looking up. And it's always good when things are looking up. Over and out."

"Some friend," Hughes said with a derisive huff.

But Lester's comments stuck with me. I mean, I was glad to know they found the murder weapon, that there was no doubt left who did it. That the case could be properly closed. But to end it by telling me things are looking up.

Could that be a message?

Things are looking up.

I smiled and glanced up, worried that Hughes had been looking at me. But he hadn't. He was staring out over the desert. This was Carterville. We had 201 people with powers living here. I couldn't think of any that could help me right now, but there must be some, right? That was why Lester said things were looking up. He couldn't come out and say it for fear of spooking Hughes.

Hope began to warm me, but I didn't trust it. Waiting right behind hope, waiting for it to fail, is despair. And wasn't hope just taking me back to denial here? Most Carterville powers are small or strange or both. But I needed something, so I grabbed a hold of it anyway.

Things are looking up.

Could there be another layer to the message?

I could see Carterville Road below us to my right as it snaked through the forest and the hills below the San Francisco Peaks to Highway 89. An old Ford Bronco was speeding down the road and slowed when it neared our position. I could see the dot of a grey-haired head leaning out the window looking up. It had to be Martin Lester. Down the road towards town I could see other vehicles coming too.

That was the other part of the message. To keep Hughes from looking down, to keep him looking up.

"There's the Grand Canyon," I said. "Even with the sun down, it's a tiny bit easier to see from here. That jagged cut in the land. The North Rim is higher than the south and that's what you can see."

Below me there were other vehicles speeding out of Carterville. Pickups. Vans. Cars. They were planning something, but keeping Lester looking to the south was going to be hard. It's natural to look at the person talking to you, even when they are dangling from your ankle while you both float a thousand feet in the air.

"I'm just going to look at that," I said. "At the Canyon. I've been looking at it all my life. At least I won't be dying in bed. At least I'll be seeing this beauty almost all the way to the end."

"Will you shut up, Henry," he hissed, "and let me actually enjoy it."

Below us, the vehicles were coming and I tried to let the hope of my town coming to help keep me warm against the cold of despair.

TWENTY-FIVE

5:35 PM CHRISTMAS DAY. HIGH ABOVE CARTERVILLE

While seeing the desert unfold before us as the sky darkened and the scene slowly faded was spectacular and maybe even metaphorically relevant, it wasn't the last view I really wanted.

I will admit that the view was one to die for, with the peaks behind us and the high desert of Arizona before us stretching out to the Grand Canyon. The sun was well set and the colors were leaching out of the scene, the sky a vaguely blue grey, the trees on the mountain almost black against the snow, and the desert a deepening brown and a dusky red. And while I was going to die when Arnie's power faded and I tumbled from this height if whatever crazy plan that was taking place below us didn't work, I'd rather be with a friend.

I'd like to be at the diner with my best friend Frank Paulson sipping coffee—or better yet a little gin and soda—and shooting the shit.

Frank and I were born and raised in Carterville. We went

to high school together. We've both lived in this little town for almost our entire lives. Frank could take one look at me and know what I was thinking. He was there with me last night—which felt like it was a year ago—with food to keep me from being drunk and making a fool of myself with the Annie madness.

And I'd like Patty Walsh to be there too. The intriguing redhead that knew what everyone wanted before they asked. I was dating Annie when Patty came to town, but every time Annie and I were "off again" it was Patty that I wondered about.

Annie hadn't been wrong about that.

And I'd like my son to be there too. Tom is going to ASU down in Phoenix, doing premed. He wants to be a doctor. He wasn't here when the meteor hit, he was living with his mother, so he doesn't have a power. Given the tendency of the young to flee from small towns and the fact that he feels too "normal" here, he doesn't visit much.

But that was the fantasy. I don't need a view at the end, I'd like to be with my best friend, the intriguing Patty Walsh, and my son. Sipping coffee. Telling stories. Laughing.

The minutes slid by in silence as my fantasy played out. Hughes and I floated over the juniper tree forest and stared out at the darkening desert and the distant and fading cut of the Grand Canyon.

I didn't look down, not overtly. I didn't want to draw his attention to the vehicles below. There was a caravan of them and they were tracking us along the road. We were close to the edge of the zone of influence. It's a sharp boundary. One moment you have powers and the next you don't. I can feel it every time I pass through it. It's like this background hum disappears, and I often breathe a sigh of relief.

I'm sure some of it's psychological. Living in Carterville where the strange and unusual is an everyday occurrence can be kind of nerve wracking. Well, when you have my job. But it's more than that. When I leave the zone of influence, my power is gone. And that is often a relief.

Yes, I love my town, but like with most things we love, it's complicated.

"What the hell are they doing?" Hughes hissed.

My heart surged to a gallop in my chest and I was yanked out of my reverie.

"Hell if I know," I said, trying to keep my words as casual as I could. The caravan, led by Lester's Bronco, was veering off the road heading out into the desert, the vehicles winding between the juniper and piñon trees, the snow here only in patches under the trees, dust kicking up in their wake. They were ahead of us now and hard not to see.

"Shit. Shit. Shit," Hughes intoned. He hadn't thought about the town and the powers there, if someone could do something to stop what seemed so inevitable. We had been up here over an hour. It both felt a lot shorter and a lot longer, but it wasn't a lot of time for people to gather and plan. What could they be doing?

I saw mattresses hanging out of some of the pickup trucks which just seemed laughable. Were they going to spread them out over the land between the trees and hope we fell on one of them? As if that would do much. I couldn't exactly get to my phone and look up the math around terminal velocity, but I knew we'd be going way too fast for a mattress to matter.

"Maybe they're coming out for the show," I said, trying to

keep my voice calm. It was a lame attempt to redirect, but besides shooting him—which would be satisfying but unhelpful—what else was I going to do?

He was staring at them, his brow furrowed. It seemed clear that he was trying to get up the courage to drop us now, drop us here before they could do anything.

"Who else did you rip off with your insurance scam?" I asked.

He stared down at me. "You are not surviving this, Henry. What the hell does it matter?"

I shrugged. It was really weird that I could do that. Because I was touching the skin of his leg, gravity wasn't having its normal effect. It wasn't like I was standing on the ground or anything, but it wasn't like I was dangling from his leg either. "Consider it my last wish." He gave me a derisive snort so I added, "It's the least you can do. We both know the mattresses won't help."

He sighed and looked back out over the desert. Below people turned on their headlights and spilled out of their vehicles and started hauling mattresses. We were too high up for me to identify everyone there, but I saw Lester get out of the Bronco and Mary Reilly was there—no mistaking that head of white hair on the short women. Deputy Ortega was there, and I saw the round-bellied and shaved-head Frank Paulson with the red-haired Patty Walsh.

That gave me pause. They are the ones I would want to be with if I knew I was going to die, but I didn't want them to see me die here and now. Not like this. Not slamming into the ground—or a couple of mattresses—at a hundred miles an hour.

"Why not," Hughes said above me. "My scam shouldn't

have worked on anyone, but the trusting Lila was easy. After that, her neighbor Emily Underwood at the antique shop asked me about the 'cash discount.'" Hughes did one of those derisive snorts again, and I really did want to shoot him. "Who would fall for that crap? It wouldn't have gone further, but Emily asked me."

"Who would fall for it?" I asked. As I thought about it, I realized that under slightly different circumstances I might have fallen for it. The police department is a business with the same budgetary challenges of all businesses. Being a cop, the scam wouldn't have worked on me—I'm too damned jaded— but I could see how if it was coming from someone you trusted in your small town you just might go for it.

"Your buddy Frank wanted the cash discount, too," he said and now I vowed to shoot him on the way down. "I swear to you, Henry, after Lila, they all came to me. They all wanted to give me cash and…" He trailed off staring out over the desert. At least he wasn't looking down anymore. They were arranging mattresses and it looked like they were dragging a deflated bounce house out of a van.

This was their plan? Mattresses and a bounce house? I stifled a groan because I didn't want Hughes to notice.

"And…" he continued above me. "I just couldn't stop. They gave me envelopes full of cash. What the hell was I supposed to do?"

"You should have earned the trust they gave you," I said, the words leaping out of me. "You should have paid their damn bills. You should have cared for the people of your community." I clamped my mouth shut. I shouldn't have said any of it. And on the surface, it might seem ridiculous that multiple folks fell for this, but it wasn't really that far-fetched.

Not in Carterville. Not in a small town where trust is key. Where watching out for each other when the world is so curious about you is required.

But I said too much. Hughes looked down. "Don't be so goddamn holy, Henry Carter. You are far from…" His mouth gaped open. "What *are* they doing?"

"Tilting at windmills," I said, letting my doubt leak out and keeping the hope in. There were fifty people down there trying to save us. The town had come together on Christmas Day to do what seemed to be impossible.

"Well, it's not going to work," he said.

Back in town, with the tall fir tree in the middle of the Carterville Circle, with snow still on the ground and the historic building perched on the hill, with the mountain as a backdrop, is what looks like the perfect Christmas snow globe. Below us was the real thing. A town coming together to try to do the impossible.

But could they?

TWENTY-SIX

5:49 PM CHRISTMAS DAY. HIGH ABOVE CARTERVILLE

THE CRIMES OF ARNOLD HUGHES WERE MOSTLY THE CRIMES OF a coward. You could argue the murder of Lila Chang was not cowardly, but it was. He resorted to violence in a fit of passion to try to avoid the consequences of what he had done.

And avoiding the consequences of your own actions is the very definition of cowardice.

I don't say that with any particular malice. We are all cowards sometimes. It is part of being human.

But Hughes had made a real run of it. And this death he was trying to execute was cowardly too. Waiting until we left the zone of influence of Carterville powers and letting it just happen. Dragging me along so he doesn't have to die alone.

But we all die alone, don't we? While we are still alive, it's nice to have loved ones with us, but the dying part? That's just us. In that moment of death, we are as completely alone as we can be.

I'm not sure if Hughes figured that out, or he wanted to make sure the rescue attempt failed, or he wanted the perverse satisfaction of taking another life, but he raised his foot. He was going to kick me off of him.

I was emblematic of what had gone wrong with his life. I was the stand-in for his failures and his cowardice and he wanted me gone. I could see it in the fierceness of his green eyes, in the rage that had taken over his face.

He pulled his foot up and paused for just a moment. "Goodbye, Henry," he hissed.

I had cycled through the five stages of grief, and in that moment, I experienced acceptance. I didn't let go or anything, but for just a moment I could accept the inevitable. That this might be a terrifying way to die, the long, hard fall to the ground, but it wouldn't last long. It would be a lot better than cancer or some kind of debilitating disease.

It was like my mind finally accepted its mortality with grace.

"See you in hell, Arnold," I said cheerfully.

His leg started its downward trajectory and the moment of acceptance fled. I wanted to live. I tightened my grip on his leg and tried to pull my head out of the way.

Then a voice floated through the air from below us. A female voice filled with the gravel of age. A world-weary voice. "Arnold Hughes, stop!"

It wasn't loud, in fact it was hard to hear, but Hughes stopped, his left leg suspended just above my head.

Mary Reilly.

I looked down and saw that she was looking up with something in front of her face. It must have been a bullhorn.

Mary Reilly. The little old lady that had a superpower. Of course. Why hadn't I thought of Mary?

Around her the residents of Carterville were scurrying like tiny ants, but Mary stood still, staring up alongside Martin Lester.

"Come down, Arnold," she continued. "Come down quickly and safely. Do it now."

I could feel her power, this tug, this desire, this pressure wrapping around my brain, this need to do as she asked. And her power wasn't even directed at me. Her power was the power of a mother to get her children to mind her. It was maternal and primal and potent and hard to ignore. This was why I always kept Mary close. If she went bad, like Arnold Hughes had, it wouldn't be pretty.

I looked up at Hughes and his face was contorted in pain. He was fighting her. "Do it!" I shouted at him. I didn't know if my words would have any effect, but being this close to Mary's power—and wanting to survive—made it so I had to act. I had to try to get him to do what she was asking him to. "Take us down!"

It was hard to tell at first. Were we going down? Were the trees and the people getting closer? And then I could tell that we were. Hughes was still fighting it. Grunting. Sweating. Cursing under his breath. Looking like he might pop a blood vessel. But Mary Reilly could not be denied for long.

For a moment, I wondered at the bounce house and the mattresses. They had laid out the mattresses, stacked them several thick, and put the bounce house on top. They were inflating it now, the rattle of the generator reaching us.

I wondered why Mary hadn't tried this earlier when we

weren't close to the edge of the zone of influence. And then it hit me. They didn't know if Mary's power would work. Whether we were too far away or we wouldn't hear her.

Hope filled me up and I dared to smile as it became clear we were going down.

"That's it, Arnold," Mary said. "Keep going. Come down to the ground quickly and safely."

But then a breeze kicked up from the north and started pushing us faster toward the edge of the zone of influence.

They must have noticed it too because Mary said, "Faster, Arnold. Come down as quickly as you can and be safe."

Above me Hughes was groaning and grunting, sweat running down his red face. He was fighting hard and it was having an effect. We were coming down but certainly not as quickly as we could be.

And then the breeze became a wind and then the wind became strong and Hughes cackled above me. We were still about seven hundred feet in the air. There was no surviving the fall, not even with a bounce house and a few layers of mattresses.

I don't know if this was real, but it felt like I could feel the edge of the zone of influence coming, the background noise of my own power fading. It seemed like maybe Hughes could too. His cackling turned positively manic and I could see why. The wind had pushed us off our course and we were not going to pass over the bounce house mattresses arrangement.

The bounce house was almost inflated, just a simple rectangle in red and blue looking so out of place in the middle of the juniper-piñon forest. But it was in the wrong spot. It would do us no good.

Hughes was positively losing it above me, his laughter

ringing out making him sound like some utterly insane comic book villain. But we were going down faster, like he wasn't fighting Mary's power so much anymore.

And then there were no powers.

I felt the background hum of my own power turn off like a switch. And then we were falling, nothing but trees and the hard earth below us.

There was no acceptance as I fell. My own scream joined Hughes's manic laughter. I let go of his leg and spread my arms out like some sky diver. Seriously. I don't know what I was thinking, but part of me wanted to do anything I could to slow the fall.

The air was cold and my descent produced a roaring wind that filled my ears and froze my face. My unzipped jacket flapped loudly around me.

Through it all I heard a woman scream, and I felt a gentle tug on my body.

What?

When we fell, we had been moving away from the bounce house topped mattresses, but along with the scream I felt that motion reverse.

The ground was rushing up, the wind was roaring, but I was moving towards the landing zone.

Time didn't slow down and my life didn't flash before my eyes. That heart-pounding fall only took a few seconds, the air filled with the woman's scream, Hughes's cackling, and my own scream.

I was moving towards the bounce house, but it wasn't going to be enough. I was going to land on the hard ground or be speared by the branches of a juniper tree.

In the last moment, the woman's scream became

agonizing and I felt the pull increase as I was jerked over the bounce house.

I came crashing down through the bounce house and on to the mattresses. Unbearable pain erupted in my body and I knew nothing.

TWENTY-SEVEN
6:02 PM CHRISTMAS DAY. NEAR CARTERVILLE

As consciousness returned, sharp pain lanced through my body, but I smiled. I was alive. Someone, a woman, had used their powers and changed my trajectory. I ran the scream I'd heard back through my mind and knew who it was.

"Annabelle," I said… or tried to say. The pain was too much and it came out more like "Aaaaa."

While Arnold Hughes had the power of levitation, Annabelle Unger was telekinetic, but only for small objects. She had overextended herself yanking my bulk back to safety.

"Don't try to talk, darlin'," Annabelle said. "We got Smitty. You're gonna to be okay."

But she didn't sound right, her voice thin and weak. Like she was in her nineties not her fifties.

I couldn't see anything, my face buried in the plastic of the bounce house, but at least I could breath. Kind of. Pain lanced through me with every breath and my exhale had a gurgly sound. How many broken ribs did I have? My heart was pounding hard, the beat irregular and I couldn't feel my feet. I felt a warm trickle of blood at my chest.

I may have been alive, but I wasn't going to be for long.

I heard other voices around me and Lester yelling at them to get back.

"You're gonna owe me, you hear me, Chief?" It was Winston "Smitty" Smith. I recognized his wispy, nasally voice.

I grunted, it was all I could do, and then I felt it. The warmth of Smitty's power. It felt like the first rays of sunshine after a long, cold storm. It felt like coming home after being away too long. It felt like my mom giving me chocolate chip cookies fresh out of the oven when I was a little kid.

Smitty had a true superpower and he used it to his advantage. Charging exorbitant fees or demanding outrageous favors.

And I could kind of see why. It was an amazing power, but it cost him. His scraggly blond hair going to grey even though he was in his early thirties. His tall, angular form perpetually gaunt.

But he was greedy, wanting as much as he could get.

I would have to pay his price, but at least I would be alive.

I groaned and lapsed back into unconsciousness.

———

WHEN CONSCIOUSNESS NEXT RETURNED, I FELT WORSE. KIND of. The pain wasn't as sharp, but it was everywhere. Like I had been shoved into a giant dryer and tumbled for a day or two. Or like I had fallen out of the sky onto a bounce house and a bunch of mattresses.

But my heartbeat was steady and I could feel my legs. I heard the distant warble of a siren growing closer. I sucked cold winter air into my lungs, feeling like it was the most precious thing in the world, glad to still be breathing.

"Come on now, Chief," Lester said as I felt hands gently roll me over. "Let's see what kind of a job old Smitty did."

"Are you sure?" another voice asked. Female and young. Deputy Ortega. "I mean… how's he even alive? He had to hit this at over a hundred miles an hour."

"I'm fine," I lied. I wasn't fine. My body was beat enough to match my emotions and my spirit. It had been a hell of a few days. I shook off Lester's hands and slowly pushed myself up.

It was one of the hardest things I had ever done. Smitty may have saved my life, but he didn't heal me anymore than he needed to.

I sucked more wonderfully cold air into my lungs and pushed my body up. No sharp pain, but the diffuse, ubiquitous pain was almost more than I could bear. Like every bone and every muscle had been bruised. Like every tendon and ligament had been strained. Like my lungs had a quarter of their former capacity and my heart was undersized for my body.

It took time and a lot of groaning, but I got myself into a sitting position and looked around. Much of my town was there, the headlights of all the vehicles driving back the deepening darkness. Frank and Patty were up on the platform of mattresses with Lester and Ortega, looks of concern on their faces. Past them I could see Mary Reilly and Annabelle, and beyond them Smitty slowly walking away, his gait that of an old man not a young one.

"There you are," Lester said with a smile, putting my

cowboy hat on my head. I felt this strange wash of relief. It had been found. It was back on my head. I felt like me again. It was like this small thing made it seem like the world, and me, could be right again… some day.

Past him, I could see that our doctor, Jenny Lion, had just arrived and was striding over towards me.

"Don't move!" she shouted.

I grunted and moved to get up, but it was just too much. "Smitty," I said by way of explanation.

"I don't care," she said as she got up on the platform, sloshing over through the deflated bounce house, a grim look on her round face.

She squatted down and brushed her brown bangs out of her eyes and gave me the look, her face scrunching in pain and her eyes going out of focus. It didn't take long, but despite the cold, sweat beaded on her forehead and she went ashen.

"Jesus, Joseph, and Mary," she gasped.

"What?" I asked. Behind her the sound of the siren was close.

Her brown eyes came back into focus and the look of surprise and compassion she gave me made think that Smitty hadn't done the job.

"I didn't know Smitty could do that," she said.

"Do what?" Ortega asked.

"Heal someone as far gone as he was," she said.

A wave of dizziness passed through me and I suddenly remembered I wasn't the only one that fell out of the sky. "Hughes?" I asked.

Lester's eyes darkened and he shook his head. "Annabelle couldn't pull you both this far. Not enough left for Smitty to work with."

I blinked, trying to take it all in.

"Am I going to live?" I asked the doctor.

She nodded. "If you take it easy for a few weeks."

I chuckled, it was a weak sound, almost a cough. I was not leaving this town without a chief of police for a few weeks. Not with the mess from Lila's murder, Hughes's crimes, and Karen Winslow's greed. "Lester, get me home."

I didn't see it, but the doc gave Lester a look that made him step back, and then she looked back at me, her brown eyes fierce. "I know you are a tough guy and all, Chief, but I see evidence of eight different broken bones, a punctured lung, and a lacerated liver. Not to mention a fair amount of internal bleeding and all the bruising and trauma. If you don't get in that ambulance and go to the hospital, I don't know if what Smitty did will be enough. Can't Officer Lester handle things for a while?"

I chuckled again and this time it sounded more like wheezing. "Didn't you hear," I said. "He's retiring. Effective immediately." I stared at Lester and he gave me a small nod. I should fire him for withholding his involvement with Lila, much less breaking out of that cell and stalking Arnold Hughes, which I should arrest him for.

"Then Annabelle," Jenny offered.

"We'll work it out," Annabelle offered. "I'll woman the office and the sheriff can cover calls for us."

"Sure," Deputy Ortega offered. "I'd like to get back out here more. Nice little town. You should go take care of yourself, Boss."

I laughed—or tried to—when Ortega said "nice little town." What the hell was this girl's definition of "nice"? I ended up coughing, the sound of it too wet for comfort.

"Okay," I said. "Okay. But I'm walking out of here. Lester, help me up."

Jenny was about to speak, but I gave her a look, one that said I would not be carried out of here on a stretcher in front of half of Carterville. She nodded. With Lester on one side and Ortega on the other—the girl was as strong as she looked—they got me up.

My vision swam and I heard a rushing sound in my ears, but I stayed conscious. Barely. There were cheers and clapping as I made my way to the two paramedics that were carrying a stretcher between the trees towards us.

"Hell of a Christmas," I said. "No one will ever forget this Carterville Christmas."

"You got that right, Boss," Ortega said.

PART 4

AFTER: NEW YEAR'S DAY

TWENTY-EIGHT

THE FLAGSTAFF MEDICAL CENTER CONFIRMED EVERYTHING Doctor Lion had told me. And then some. I truly owed Smitty, and all those people that had dragged their mattresses and that bounce house out into the forest, my life.

And I especially owe Annabelle. If I had hit the ground, that would have been it. A very quick death just like Arnold Hughes received. Her overuse of her powers cost her. She had a migraine for five days and hasn't been able to use her powers since.

But the hospital only kept me overnight and sent me home. Which was almost worse. My sister, Wendy, who shares the original Carter home with me, is a nurse. She fussed. A lot. But at least I could sleep.

And in some ways that wasn't great either. At least the waking up. For a moment before my brain got back into gear, it was like I was still living my old life. Annie and I were in the middle of a lovely "on again" phase, Lila was serving coffee down at PGC, and Arnold Hughes was someone I hardly ever had to deal with.

That moment wouldn't last, and then reality would come crashing down on me, another wave of grief flattening me, and I would feel hollow and alone.

I'd like to say that I'm too old for feelings like that, but the hard times are all about equal opportunity. Age doesn't matter. The hard times are always available.

I'm old enough to know that I was grieving. The loss of my friend. The loss of my relationship. The loss of Martin Lester as my partner on the job. But that didn't make it any easier.

It was a hell of a change and I needed the rest, but I'm just no good at doing nothing. After a few days, I started going down to the office. Only twenty minutes the first time, and I needed a nap, but a little more each day.

I was down there on New Year's Day, feeling the tiniest sliver of hope, thinking that maybe a fresh year was just what I needed. A chance to begin again.

I was in my closet of an office banging on the keyboard and looking through files when Karen Winslow walked in.

There was snow clinging to her fancy fur-lined snow boots and a dusting on her shoulders as she took off her over-priced fur-edged parka.

"Good to see you up and about, Henry," she said, leaning against the open doorway to my office, the floral note of her expensive perfume wafting in. I didn't wrinkle my nose, but I sure didn't like it.

"Good to be seen, Karen," I said. "What can I do for you?"

"Just saw the CPD vehicle out front and thought it might be you," she said with a smile on her lean face. The smile looked genuine, which wasn't to be trusted. She was a politician. "How are you?"

I smiled back and I can guarantee you that my smile was fake. "I see the renovation has started," I said, ignoring her question. "When will the Carterville Brewery open? Spring maybe?"

And, yes, I was still pissed. Karen Winslow wasn't the murderer and she had broken no laws, but she had broken something in our relationship.

"No firm date," she said, her smile growing. I could almost see the dollar signs behind her hazel eyes. "We're going to do it right. We're going to make Carterville proud."

"Glad to hear it," I lied, and started shifting through the paperwork on my desk. The sheriff's deputies had made a few arrests last night and I needed to look over the paperwork. Just disturbing the peace and the usual New Year's Eve nonsense.

"Listen, Henry," she said, her tone changing so quickly I looked back up and saw the smile melting into a frown. "I hate to be the bearer of bad tidings, especially today, but the town council has been talking and…"

She bit her lip and I could almost see her as a teenage girl, still shy and not quite sure of herself. Probably when she started doing the French braid in her blond hair and wearing that awful perfume.

"I'm a big boy, Karen," I said. "Just spit it out."

She nodded and took a deep breath. "There are some on the council that are talking about defunding the Carterville Police Department."

My jaw dropped open and I couldn't hide my shock.

"The Coconino County Sheriff already does some work

for us. We have a contract with them," she said, licking her lips. "Some are saying why not just contract them for all of our policing needs." She stared at me, trying to read my face, but my jaw was shut and I just stared back. "It makes sense economically," she said.

I kept staring. It was totally clear that by "some are saying" she meant "*I* am saying."

"This whole business with Officer Lester and..." she continued. "Well... It has left a bad taste. If you know what I mean."

I nodded slowly. "Martin has retired," I said. "His house is up for sale and he's decided to leave town. So that should help with the 'bad taste.'"

"Still..." she said.

I sighed and motioned for her to sit down. It was awkward with her in the doorway towering over me, and I didn't have the energy to stand.

She nodded and sat, the delay giving me just enough time to think.

"Look, Karen," I said. "I get it. Believe me, I get it. The fact that one of the town council members was stealing from us and committed murder has rocked this town. We are all feeling it. We all want change, something that feels hopeful, that feels like this kind of thing won't happen again."

And, yes, I was turning it back on her. Arnold Hughes had been close with Karen. And, let's face it, what Lester did was nothing compared to Hughes.

"So you'll support the move?" she asked, ignoring my jab at the council.

I made a show of thinking about it. Like it was a viable

idea. I know I've said I hate politics, but I have learned to play the game.

"Deputy Ortega did well helping with the whole Chang mess," she offered. "It's a hopeful sign that their office can adapt to our needs."

I smiled and nodded, fishing some paperwork out of the pile. "Isabella Ortega," I said, scanning the document. "Twenty-four years old. Born in Farmington, New Mexico. Graduated from NAU with a degree in Criminology and Criminal Justice. Speaks Spanish and Navajo fluently." I looked up. "You're right," I said. "She did do well and, for reasons beyond me, liked it here. With Martin stepping away, I need another officer. This is her job application. I'm just about to offer her the job."

Minute traces of emotion passed over Karen's face. Surprise, anger, and a few I couldn't recognize.

I leaned forward and said, "And while I do recognize using the sheriff might be a little easier on the budget, I don't think it takes into account Carterville's special needs and special population. Consistency really counts here."

She gave me a thin-lipped smile. "Well, I'm afraid there are those on the council that don't agree with that."

I shrugged. "I trust the council will make a wise decision with due deliberation."

"Very well, Henry," she said as she stood up. "I just didn't want you hearing it via the rumor mill."

I nodded. "Thanks for that." When she was at the door, I said, "One more thought."

She turned, her face hopeful.

"If you do defund the CPD, I'll be out of a job despite my position being an elected one," I said with a smile.

"I am sorry to say that would be the case," she said. And I'm sure she wouldn't be sorry.

"If that were the case, I'd have a lot of time on my hands," I said. "I'd have to find something else to do."

Her brow furrowed as she studied me. "Do you have something in mind, Henry?"

I shrugged. "I don't know. I could take a shot at running for mayor. I mean, I'm fairly popular around here and I suspect some of the business owners might like having a mayor that is not in competition with them."

It was time for her jaw to drop open.

To be honest, I had zero desire to run for mayor, much less be mayor. But Karen wouldn't think that. She's a political animal and thinks everyone else is just like her.

Her surprise didn't last long. "Well, we'll just have to see how it all plays out, won't we?"

"That we will," I said.

I chuckled after she left. I was pretty damn sure that was the end of that idea, and at least there was one fun thing happening today, because I knew the rest of the day would not even have the pleasure of besting the mayor.

TWENTY-NINE
10:15 AM NEW YEAR'S DAY. CARTERVILLE CHURCH

I HATE FUNERALS.

Don't get me wrong. I get the need for them. The why. I've even felt the benefits of them. Closure is desperately important, but the whole affair is much too emotionally oriented for me. And there is often this liberal rewriting of history where you focus only on the good parts of a person's life and maybe a few of the more amusing wrinkles in their personality, but you leave the bigger flaws and the bad stuff behind.

It makes sense. Don't speak ill of the dead and all of that. Remember the best of those that are gone. But I've been to plenty of funerals where I had to wonder who the hell we were talking about.

I suspect my funeral will be a bit like that with folks glossing over my obvious flaws to focus on the good that I managed to do despite myself. But not Lila Chang. That was not needed at her funeral. She had her past, the one most of us didn't know much about but knew she was hiding from, but otherwise she was a lovely person that made the world a better place. The world seemed a bit dimmer without her in it.

My world seemed significantly dimmer without her in it.

And looking at all that I've written here, that might be worthy of questioning. The whole were we friends bit. The fact that there was so much about her life that I didn't know. Annie Smith saying she was part of my "Carterville harem."

The truth is there were many things about Lila that I didn't know. So many. But I knew that our interactions brightened my day. That our relationship, just as it was, had a measurable positive impact on my life. That my heart ached at the loss of her and my mind kept seeing her dead body slumped against that tree when I closed my eyes.

Justice, such as it is, had been done. Arnold Hughes was dead and wouldn't be hurting anyone else, but those scales were far from balanced.

It was standing room only in the church at the top of Carter Hill. The inside of it was just like the outside, made of rough volcanic rock gathered from the vicinity. The ceiling was thirty feet above us and the room had the feel of a cave. Tall stained-glass windows let light in and there were wooden pews polished by over a century of parishioners.

Most of the town had turned out for the service. There were flowers and a large picture of Lila up front crowding around a small table that held a simple clay urn that contained her remains.

The air was cold and the sound of sniffing echoed in the large space. Most folks still had their jackets on, it took the heater a long time to warm the air in here, not that it was ever warm in winter.

I was sitting in the first row with Martin Lester to my left and Frank Paulson to my right. Lester was hunched over not meeting anyone's eyes.

I'm sure it was the grief that kept him hunched over but probably some form of shame too. Carterville was a small town, so everyone knew all the sordid details at this point. About Lila and his baby. About Arnold Hughes and his crimes. About Annie and my breakup and Hughes's part in that.

Pastor Lisa had done her bit with bible verses and prayers and had just opened it up for us to share. Lisa Bass led our one and only church and had a kind way about her. She preached, but gently, and she didn't make it all about her. For a service like this, she just tried to set the stage and give the rest of us time to share and grieve.

"I know we are all feeling this one," she said, her deep voice filling the space with ease. She wore a simple black skirt and blouse with a sweater over it, her tight black curls swept back, a smile on her oval face, her eyes a lovely brown and her skin a shade darker. "But who will get this started? We all loved Lila, surely one of you is bold enough to take the first step."

At the other end of the pew, I saw Karen Winslow stir and I'd be damned if I would let her set the direction here. I stood up quickly and cleared my throat. A small wave of dizziness passed through me, but I kept it from showing.

"Please, Chief," Pastor Lisa said. "Get us started."

I nodded and looked around at my town. I knew every face in the room. Their names. Their pasts. What they did. And in many cases, their hopes for the future.

"Lila Chang was my friend," I began, my voice scratchy

and weak. I took a deep breath and said it again. "Lila Chang was my friend. I didn't know her nearly was well as I would have liked. And not nearly as well as she deserved. But that didn't matter to Lila. She was always this bright light there behind her steel monster serving up coffee and making everyone's day better."

There were nods and sniffs and mumbled agreement.

"You might be wondering how can a single person have such a large effect on a town by mostly slinging coffee?" I asked. "It's not *what* she did. It's *how* she did it. It's the joy she brought to every single day that was contagious. It's the way she was there for you even when it was a bad day for her. Even when she was scared."

Lester was looking up at me, tears in his pale blue eyes, and he gave me a small nod. Like he wanted me to keep going. Like he wanted me to say the words he couldn't.

"I'll be honest with you all," I continued. "On Christmas Eve, I failed her. I failed to be her friend and I failed to do my job. I won't go into specifics, because I'm sure you all know what was going on." There were some nervous chuckles and Annie Smith glared at me from the back of the church. "But I was having a bad night. And so was Lila. But she was the one trying to make me feel better. She was the one trying to hold me up."

I looked down, feeling my own guilt and shame. I wasn't worried about telling the truth here. This was the time for it, and besides, I'm sure there were many that were thinking it, so why not say it.

"And that right there," I continued. "The way Lila was a part of our community, always giving, always thinking of others, is what makes a town like Carterville work. It's what makes a town like ours worth living in."

I looked around and people were quiet now, but I saw some nodding. "Her death is a tragedy. Make no mistake about that. And I sure hope there is a heaven, and if there is, I'm sure Lila is there showing them a thing or two. But, I think what will define us individually and as a town is what we do with this tragedy.

"Do we let it be and just move on? Or do we learn the lessons that Lila taught us and try to be better. Try to help more. Try to make this a better place to live?"

There were a lot of serious looks. I wasn't telling a cute story or sharing a fun little anecdote. I was challenging them. I suddenly felt hot and didn't particularly like some of the hard gazes on me. From Karen Winslow. From Smitty. From Annie Smith.

"That's how we honor her," I continued. "That's how we use the pain of the tragedy and do something good with it." I took a deep breath. "That's what I'm going to do. I'm going to try to be more like Lila. To remember her by trying to live up to the example she set."

I sat down, my cheeks flushing. Lester was looking at his lap but he grabbed my hand and squeezed it hard. Frank gave me a grim nod, tears pooling in his bright blue eyes.

Mary Reilly stood up next and shared a cute story about when she and William had had Lila over for dinner. It went from there, and I listened to the stories and learned more about my friend. Lila liked to crochet, although I have no idea how that is different than knitting. She was a wiz at Scrabble and terrible at Trivial Pursuit but was an ardent practitioner of game night. She was a dog person but never got a dog since running PGC took so much.

And on it went. I let the details wash over me and deepen the picture of Lila in my mind. We knew her real name now, it was Ella, but she would always be Lila to us. I was happy to know these details, but I regretted not spending more time with her and I was still angry that her life had been snatched away. I still felt the shame of failing her. But the laughter and the tears, and the fact that we did it together, was cleansing.

THIRTY

11:40 AM NEW YEAR'S DAY. CARTERVILLE CHURCH

I LINGERED IN THE CHURCH AFTER MOST EVERYONE HAD LEFT. Pastor Lisa was bustling around, putting hymnals in their place and cleaning up. Her movements echoed in the big space now that it was mostly empty.

I was chilled from sitting so long in the cool air and my stomach gnawed with hunger from not eating enough today. The wake would be starting down at the Carterville Diner and there would be food and coffee aplenty, but still I didn't move.

My strength had faded and I felt wrung out.

What I had said to everyone lingered in my mind. I had failed Lila. To make her death worth something, I had to do better. But how? I am as human as the next person. I had a job that was often overwhelming. I had a life I needed to rebuild and rethink now that Annie was out of the picture.

I sighed and pushed myself up and turned and found that there was one person left in the church. Annie Smith.

Her piercing blue eyes were drilling into me and she slowly stood. "Well," she said, her voice loud and echoing around the stone building. "At least your harem is one person smaller now."

The shock of her statement almost knocked the wind out of me and I felt my cheeks flush hot. I opened my mouth to bark something back, but shut it and slowly walked towards Annie, studying her. Her black hair, her high cheekbones, her petite form. She was in a black dress with a coat on top of it, but I knew every curve underneath and part of me still longed for her.

As I approached her, I smiled. The words had been sharp, they had been meant to wound, but it was like lancing an abscess. It hurt. Like hell. But I felt relief now, like I could heal.

"I know you, Annie," I said gently. "You don't really mean that."

She opened her mouth to speak but I took her face in my hands and that stopped her. I don't know whether it was the holy place we were in or my dedication to be a better person, but I could see things much clearer than I usually could.

"I think you said that so there's no going back," I said. "So we will never get back together."

Her eyes widened and surprise rippled across her face.

I let my hands drop. "But you don't have to worry about that, Annie. We are through."

She looked embarrassed, briefly, and then sighed and nodded. "Arnie," she said as if that one word could contain her brutal infidelity and explain everything. Could wash away the asymmetry of our mistakes that day, where I ran to Lila for a gift and she slept with another man.

I shook my head. "We would have gotten over that… eventually."

Her brow furrowed, making her look more her age. "What?" she asked.

I shrugged. "You know we would have," I said. "It might have taken a year, but we would have healed. We would have ended up back together again."

"But…" she began. "But you just said we are through. If not Arnie then… why?"

Even in that holy space, even with my clear mind, a part of me was enjoying her confusion.

I stared at her, studying her beautiful face. She was my first great passion back in high school. And this town being as small as it is, she may be my last. Part of me thought I owed her the truth. Part of me thought it would be cruel to say. Both of those parts of me drove me to say it.

"Because, Annie," I said. "When I saw Lila's dead body for the first time, you were who came to my mind. And again for a little bit there, after Arnold challenged your story, I thought you were the murderer. And that meant I thought you were capable of doing something like that. I can't… I…" I felt the unnecessary cruelty of the words as they were coming out and couldn't go any further, but it was too late.

The color drained from her face and her mouth sagged open.

The words, once they were out, made my stomach churn. It was the truth. I couldn't look at her the same way anymore. But I should have let the reason be Arnie and left it at that. I felt my cheeks flush red just as Annie slapped me. Hard. The sound of it echoing in the big space and a gasp coming from Pastor Lisa.

"Fuck you, Henry Carter," she said. She turned and stormed off.

THIRTY-ONE
11:54 AM NEW YEAR'S DAY. CARTERVILLE OVERLOOK

I KNEW BETTER. SOMETIMES THE TRUTH IS NOT THE BEST THING. It seems like it should be, but it's not. The world has never been that black and white, it's always been shades of grey. So many shades of grey.

Annie was gone and I stood at the overlook staring out at the view. I was drained and exhausted, hoping that seeing the desert would revive me.

The sky was laden with high clouds and the wind had whipped up the dust in the desert, so the view wasn't as good as it gets. I couldn't quite make out the cut of the Grand Canyon, and it was bothering me.

I knew where it was. I knew it was there. But I couldn't see it. As if that made a difference. I know it was my recovering body and my recent encounter with Annie that was spooking me, but it felt like something was wrong. Horribly wrong.

And, yeah, Lila Chang and Arnold Hughes were dead. Martin Lester was packing up to leave. Those things were all very wrong. Our town would heal, I would heal, but it would take time and neither of us would be quite the same.

It occurred to me then that I still didn't know what Lila's power was. She claimed, just like I do, that she didn't have a power. But I am sure that she did.

Maybe it was something about her that just seemed so natural. Like remembering everyone's order or what item in her shop someone longed for. Or maybe it was far afield like being a lucid dreamer and being able to live whatever kind of life she wanted when she was asleep. Or something I can't even imagine.

But I'm glad I don't know. Our powers don't define us—or at least they shouldn't—and I want to remember my kind, thousand-watt-smile friend just like she was.

"Shit view today, eh?" someone said next to me and I jumped.

It was Smitty, his sharp features pointed out at the desert. I had been so lost in my own thoughts I hadn't heard him walk up.

"It's always a good view," I said, turning back to the desert. "Even on the worst days."

The chill from the service had deepened now that I was outside. I should go home and warm up. I could sure use a stiff drink. But it felt like if I left, things would get even more real.

Lila's service was over and that made her death more real. My face still felt the sting of Annie's slap and that made our breakup more real. I had almost died, and giving into the fatigue I still felt would make that more real.

And reality wasn't what I wanted. I needed a little distraction and a lot of denial. Just for a while. Just so I could heal some more. But what I had was Smitty and it was clear he wanted something.

"Good to see you up and around," he said. He had his new age flowing robes on underneath a white down coat. He'd changed his wardrobe about six months ago and I couldn't stand it. It's like he thought his fancy powers and his fancy clothes somehow made him a different person.

Well… he was a different person. He was no longer a petty thief. He had moved on to bigger things when the meteor granted him a superpower, and I owed him.

"It's good to be up and around," I said. "Thank you, Smitty."

He glanced at me, smiled, and nodded. He was leaning on a cane made out of some reddish hardwood and tipped with silver. That seemed a bit overkill to me, him acting like he was still recovering from what he did for me. "Happy I could help," he said. "Wish I could have done a better job. You look like shit."

I nodded. "I feel like shit."

He chuckled. "And so you should. Dropping out of the clear blue sky on Christmas Day and walking away from it. You oughta go write a book or something, Henry. 'The Man that Fell from the Sky' or something like that. You've seen a lot from our little town."

I snorted. "As if I would ever have the time."

"One of these days," he said, his smile friendly but his words chilling.

"How much would it take to pay my debt to you?" I asked.

And, yes, it was an abrupt change in conversation, but I had no desire to trade pleasantries with Smitty. He wanted something, so we best get to it.

"Fifty K," he said without missing a beat, smiling and showing off his over-bleached teeth and somehow reminding me of a shark.

I blinked and stared at him. "Jesus… Smitty… I…."

"Don't soil yourself there, Henry," he said with a derisive chuckle. "Truth is I gave you more than I've ever given anyone. You should have died. Several times over. I'm still recovering." He lifted up his cane for emphasis and he did look paler than usual.

"But… I can't," I began. "I don't have that kind of money just sitting around."

His smile widened and there was something distinctly predatorial about it. "Relax," he said. "I don't want your money. Got plenty of that. I just need to know you'll be there for me like I was there for you."

I just stared at him. "I can't heal you," I began. "I don't even have a—"

"Yeah, yeah," he said, interrupting me. "You don't have a power. But you do have *power*. You're the law around here. One day I may need you."

I opened my mouth to say more but couldn't find the words. He had healed Karen Winslow of her cancer and likely made a similar deal with her, getting the mayor on his side. Now he had the chief of police literally owing him his life.

I never liked Smitty before. At all. But in that moment, I started to hate him.

"I won't break the law for you," I said.

He smiled. It was a relaxed, easy smile. "I wouldn't dream of it, Chief. But I know you are a man of honor. I know you'll be there for me if I ever need you. And I'm almost well enough to use my powers again. Feel free to come by and I'll get you over the hump, get you back to feeling like your normal self."

He didn't give me a chance to reply but turned and walked off, leaning heavily on his cane.

I didn't know what Smitty wanted from me, but I knew it was a price I wouldn't want to pay, and I sure as hell wouldn't be going to see him again and getting further into his debt. I shrugged it off and turned back to the view. There was nothing I could do about it now.

I breathed in the cold air and was finally able to spot the cut of the Grand Canyon. I smiled and suddenly everything seemed okay. Well, as okay as it could be under the circumstances.

I didn't know it then, of course, but some seeds had been planted during this tumultuous Christmas. It would take a few years before they bore fruit, but boy would they.

WANT MORE CARTERVILLE?

There's more Carterville for you. *Destroyer of Carterville* takes place seven months after the events in this book, the conflicts and complications in this strange town heating up dramatically. There is more information on *Destroyer of Carterville* below.

The best way to find out when things happen in Carterville is to sign up for my email newsletter at RobertJMcCarter.com/newsletter. When you subscribe you'll get a free 750+ page ebook, *Bits, Bites, and Rarities: The Worlds of Robert J. McCarter*, that introduces you to my many series, and has four stories you can't read anywhere else!

Or, if you'd like a different kind of mystery, check out my *Walter Anchor, Ghost Detective* series. That's right. A ghost who solves murders. The ebook of the first case, *Detecting Haley*, is free when you sign up for my newsletter.

———

Destroyer of Carterville

CARTERVILLE, AZ. POPULATION: 290. People with powers: 200

Just a sleepy former mining town turned tourist haven in the mountains of Northern Arizona until the "incident"—the meteorite that gave everyone in the town powers, but only while in or near Carterville.

When Winston "Smitty" Smith starts receiving bizarre threats, chief of police Henry Carter will put aside their long rivalry to solve this strange case that threatens the future of Carterville itself.

With not just Henry's life on the line, but those he cares about the most, can Henry find a way out of the deadly trap set by an enemy too powerful to beat?

From Robert J. McCarter, long-time Arizona resident and the author of *The Blood of Carterville*, comes a mystery and a town you will never forget.

Get a copy today!

ACKNOWLEDGMENTS

I write a lot of fiction that takes place in Arizona, which is natural since I've spent most of my life in this state. But recently I've been writing books where location has become a bigger part of the story. This Carterville series is an example of that.

While Carterville is a fictional place, I live in Northern Arizona not too far from where Carterville is located. The feel of the land and the weather, the seasons and the views, have permeated me during all my years here. It's a beautiful place with mountains and deserts, real seasons, and lots of wide open spaces.

As such, part of what needs to be acknowledged about this book is the beauty, views, and wide open spaces of my home. So thank you Northern Arizona for always being an inspiring place to live and explore.

As always, I had plenty of other help and inspiration. To my beta readers, Roni Hornstein, Peter Klein, and Eliot Schipper, and to my proofreader, Diana Cox, thanks for making this book better.

Thanks to Elizabeth Fitzekam for starting the series bible for Carterville which helped so much in writing this book. And big thanks to my amazing wife and first listener, Aleia

O'Reilly, for your unending support on this crazy writing adventure.

And thanks to you all for reading. I hope you enjoyed your time in Carterville. There is more coming soon!

ABOUT THE AUTHOR

Robert J. McCarter is the author of more than fifteen novels and over one hundred and fifty short stories. He is a regular contributor to *Pulphouse Fiction Magazine* and his short fiction has also appeared in *The Saturday Evening Post, Andromeda Spaceways Inflight Magazine, Everyday Fiction,* and numerous anthologies.

Robert writes in a variety of genres from contemporary fantasy to science fiction and just about everything in between. His diverse background–including a career in software engineering, growing up on a ranch riding horses, and acting–colors the stories he tells.

He lives in the mountains of Arizona with his amazing wife and his ridiculously adorable dogs.

Find out more at:
RobertJMcCarter.com

BOOKS BY ROBERT J. MCCARTER

Carterville Mysteries

- **Out of a Christmas Sky**
- **Destroyer of Carterville**
- **The Blood of Carterville**
- **Faces of Carterville**
- **Return to Carterville**

Walter Anchor, Ghost Detective Stories

- **Case 1: Detecting Haley** (also part of *Life After: Stories of Life, Death, and the Places in Between*)
- **Case 2: The Ghost Bride's Gift**
- **Case 3: A Long Hard Fall**
- **Case 4: Death of a Dentist**
- **Case 5: A Hollywood Kind of a Murder**
- **Case 6: The Red Arrow Murders**
- **Unfinished Business: The Cases of Walter Anchor Ghost Detective**

For a complete list of Walter Anchor stories, go to RobertJMcCarter.com/WalterAnchor

Novels in the "Ghost's Memoir" world:

- Shuffled Off: A Ghost's Memoir, Book 1
- Drawing the Dead
- To Be a Fool: A Ghost's Memoir, Book 2

- Of Things Not Seen: A Ghost's Memoir, Book 3
- A Boy, a Girl, and a Ghost

For a complete list the "Ghost's Memoir" novels, go to ShuffledOff.com

The Woody and June versus the Apocalypse Series

Find out more at WoodyAndJune.com

The Neutrinoman and Lightningirl Series

Find out more at Neutrinoman.com

Other Novels:

- Seeing Forever
- Where the Past Belongs: An Angelica and Ash Time Travel Adventure

For a more information, go to RobertJMcCarter.com